RONALD FRAME

Ronald Frame was born in 1953 in Glasgow and educated there and at Oxford. His first published stories appeared when he was 17, but it was not until 1982, after a brief stint of teaching, that he began to write full time. The author of eleven books, including A WOMAN OF JUDAH, SANDMOUTH PEOPLE, WATCHING MRS GORDON, UNDERWOOD AND AFTER and WALKING MY MISTRESS IN DEAUVILLE, Ronald Frame is also the winner of several awards. WINTER JOURNEY, his first novel, was joint winner of the first Betty Trask Award in 1984, A LONG WEEKEND WITH MARCEL PROUST won a Scottish Arts Council Award, and PENELOPE'S HAT was shortlisted for the James Tait Black Memorial Prize and the McVitie's Scottish Book of the Year Award.

Ronald Frame has also written several television and Sony-nominated radio plays which include his radio adaptation of WINTER JOURNEY, hailed as 'of stunning brilliance . . . exciting and poignant' (*Financial Times*). He has adapted a radio memoir called GHOST CITY for BBC TV Scotland, and this will be screened in late 1993. His first television play, PARIS, won both the Samuel Beckett Award and the Television Industries' Panel's Most Promising Writer New to Television Award.

———

———

Ronald Frame

WINTER JOURNEY

sceptre

Copyright © Ronald Frame 1984

First published in Great Britain in 1984 by The Bodley Head Ltd

Sceptre edition 1993

Sceptre is an imprint of Hodder and Stoughton Paperbacks, a division of Hodder and Stoughton Ltd

British Library C.I.P.

A CIP catalogue record for this title is available from the British Library

ISBN 0-340-579730

Printed and bound in Great Britain for Hodder and Stoughton Paperbacks, a division of Hodder and Stoughton Ltd, Mill Road, Dunton Green, Sevenoaks, Kent TN13 2YA. (Editorial Office: 47 Bedford Square, London WC1B 3DP) by Cox & Wyman Ltd, Reading Berks.

There is only one history of importance, and it is the history of what you once believed in, and the history of what you came to believe in, and what cities or country you saw, and what trees you remembered.

KAY BOYLE, *White as Snow*

1

At Christmas-time in my sixth year, 1958, a revelation occurred to me on the third floor of Harrods, in the toy department.

My mother and I were at the end of a queue of frenzied parents and children waiting to be admitted to talk with Santa Claus in his grotto. The last couple in front were ushered inside.

After that there was a delay. As each minute passed, I felt more and more anxious. When I allowed myself to look at my watch at last, it said only a couple of minutes left till closing time.

I became fidgety and impatient. I thought my mother by contrast seemed rather reluctant about this piece of business ahead of us. (I'd guessed long before now – at least I was *almost* completely sure – that it was only so much hocus-pocus in the end: but the theatricality of Christmas still had the effect of setting off a cloud of butterflies inside me.)

When we were finally waved forward past the barrier I felt she was very slow off her mark, too slow if she'd *really* cared. I wondered, was she dragging her feet in their elegant crocodile shoes so that we'd be late getting to the grotto?

We reached the desk disguised as an igloo with a cut-out window in the front.

The woman inside wore a fluffy white Eskimo hood and looked thoroughly out of sorts. Even the familiar spell of my mother's hauteur and Worth perfume wasn't able to work on her.

'We *should* close at five, madam,' she said. 'Sharp.'

She undid the chain on a 'Closed' sign.

'You'll have to pay me. Usually it's a bear you pay.'

She peered down at me.

'Santa's got to feed his reindeers, young lady. It's their tea time. They're famished.'

'Rein*deer*,' I explained. 'There isn't an "s".'

The woman looked daggers at me.

'*I*'ve seen them,' she said. '*I* know what they are.'

'They're reindeer,' I confirmed for her as politely as I could. 'Like fish.'

Or sheep, I was going to suggest, but my mother sighed and, with her Sulka suede glove, she tapped me on the shoulder to go forward.

The woman craned her neck out the window as we walked in and I heard her say what she thought of me, just loudly enough for me to pick up.

'And they don't like hoity-toity kids for another thing. Makes them sick. Stuck-up little madams.'

There was no one else left when we ventured inside. I asked my mother where we were supposed to be.

'In an ice palace,' she told me.

'Oh,' I said.

I didn't feel very affected, even if it *was* a palace. Maybe that was accounted for by the woman switching off the little twinkly lights in the polystyrene walls behind us. The grotto seemed to have more atmosphere as the stalagmites and stalactites threw their long, pointed shadows on the floor, like a witch's fingers. But then in the next few seconds more plugs must have been pulled out: the fingers vanished, and when I looked up the Viewmaster pictures of Lapland you were meant to see through windows in the ice were fading to darkness.

'Oh,' I repeated with more disappointment.

The sledges you were supposed to mount to be carried in and out of the inner sanctum suddenly lurched to a squeaky halt on

8

the circle of rails. A waterfall which stopped falling at the same moment turned out to be only shredded silver paper on rollers. It became very still without the hum of all the machinery.

'I wonder where he is,' my mother said.

'Who?' I asked quite unnecessarily, just for the sake of making my own voice heard in the little night.

'Who else? Father Christmas, of course!'

I left her perched on one leg removing her Rayne shoe and walked on ahead to see, curious to discover, towards the next corner of polystyrene snow mountain and the lights on the other side of it.

Past the mountain I came upon a stuffed polar bear rearing up on its back legs. Someone had put a lost mitten in its mouth and it didn't look very pleased. It smelt a bit too: civilization and the hot electric light bulbs overhead didn't seem to be agreeing with it after a long day.

On a plinth opposite there was a life-sized waxwork of a squatting Eskimo, fishing through a hole in some papier-mâché ice. He was frozen in mid-movement, bent over his rod as if he'd fallen asleep. A walrus must have been meant to poke itself up through the hole but its hydraulics had been turned off at the mains and I could only see the matted brown dome of its head.

I was thinking that the experience wasn't really worth the four shillings each we'd had to pay to get in when I heard a grunt from somewhere near – and a watery sound, which I recognized was the dribbling of coins. I crept forward on the balls of my feet, to spy round the next corner.

Suddenly there he was: the universal myth, a vision in scarlet. It was *him*! Father Christmas! (It *was* him, I asked myself – wasn't it?)

He had his back turned to me. He was in a stooping position, inside his hallowed grotto, which was like a pergola – or a cage even – with pillars that looked as if they'd been sculpted from the royal icing Mrs Taylor made when she baked us our Christmas cake.

Still crouching, he corkscrewed himself round. His white cotton-wool beard was pushed up on a wire over his head and a cigarette dangled out of his mouth; his gown was unbuttoned to show his string vest and a bush of black hair on his chest. A trap door was flapping open in another polar bear's bottom and he had his hand up inside, pulling out money. He wasn't being at all jovial: in fact he appeared to be quite upset about something.

'How many bloody times have I told you, Freda?' he shouted through to the unpleasant woman we'd given our florins to. 'It's the mums put the money in. I've told you a hundred times. Jesus, there's half a sweetshop up this bear's bum.'

He unstuck another blockage and dislodged – I watched its descent – a coloured stream of toffees and boilings.

I made my retreat after that, very quickly.

I think my mother must have heard too because she took my hand and turned us round in the dark towards the entrance.

'But I haven't got my gift!' I said.

'We'll come another day,' she told me.

I saw she was smiling, but rather tiredly. The smile was the kind she wore for our shopping expeditions: it included everyone and no one: it was like a lighthouse beam, warning of perilous currents and rocks for anyone who might try to come too close.

'Santa's got another grotto he goes to,' she said, 'in Derry and Toms. Mrs Taylor could take you next time, when she's finished in the house. Couldn't she? I read you get more for your money there, anyway.'

I think I muttered something back, for common courtesy's sake, but I was embarrassed and awkward: and I felt it was on *her* account – for the sake of my quicksilver mother whom I had started to regard with far more caution during this year of lightning revelations, 1958, when she'd taken to veering with no warning from patience (like today) to rage (as on so many others) – I was disappointed and ashamed *for her* that she could imagine the silly, empty ritual of 'Father Christmas' was a pretence worth saving.

*　　*　　*

In the mornings he sits in a taverna. He opens up the case he carries about with him – a very battered brown leather attaché case, of the kind government officers are issued with (the tell-tale rights of ownership have been smoothed to red blotches on the lid) – and he removes a selection of books he has equipped himself with for the day: whatever in the way of paperbacks he's bought from the revolving stands in either of the big beach hotels.

He drinks coffee – the bitter Turkish variety – and stays on till lunch time, when he moves outside into the garden of olive trees. He occupies one of the tables sheltered from the full blaze of the sun. (Even so, his skin is very burnt, the veins have begun their journey upwards to the surface of his face.) He eats either fish and a salad or an egg dish with a salad. He drinks – a small measure of some fiery Greek spirit, which his stomach seems quite accustomed to.

It isn't Prunier's or Quaglino's or Claridge's Causerie or any of the other fashionable restaurants where he made the mistake of being seen dining with his wife, and too often. The chairs are slats of lurid 'Day-glo' plastic, the tables have oil-cloths over them. But it's cheap to eat like this, and in this place, and his alfresco way of life is generally healthier than that of his colleagues still working on the Whitehall treadmill.

After lunch – about two o'clock – he makes his way back (as quickly as he can manage in the boiling heat, and walking smartly for a fifty-four-year-old man), back the length of the small town to his white cottage in the fields.

The shutters are normally pulled fast across the windows. It must be to prevent the sun doing damage to the few pieces of furniture he managed to have shipped out. The specimens he has are excellent (I sneaked a look one morning, perched up on tiptoe): a Queen Anne walnut bureau bookcase, a Chippendale Chinese chair, a commode (satinwood?), a gilded sofa.

He retires inside. The door closes, and presumably he has a siesta, like the rest of the town. Usually he emerges again just after four o'clock. Most days he will walk the distance to a little public cove and there he swims: his body is healthily brown, and sinewy and lean as it always was. He lies on the pebbles in the sun, with a straw hat covering his face. Then he finds some shade and sits a while longer and reads.

On his way back to the cottage he buys his food, in shops where he is an established – but unforthcoming – customer. He exchanges cursory words with two or three people he passes in the street. (The townsfolk not employed in the shops are already beginning to gather for the preliminaries to the evening's long ritual of reminiscing and setting the world to rights.) Through a few open doorways television sets blare and he stands seeing what he can inside the gloom. There are always tourists about, idling before drinks and dinner, but he has a sixth sense for them and avoids them as soon as they come into sight. He can do it just by finding a building's shadow and moving close into the wall, taking care never to let his speed slacken. That way there is no danger of confrontation or – the worst hazard – recognition.

His residence of years hasn't given him the counterfeit look of a native, so he must continue to be careful. His tan apart, he is unmistakably English in his appearance. You could easily imagine him embarking on his retirement in a south coast fleshpot town: Torquay, or Sidmouth, or Hove. His clothes may be a little thin for that, but his face confirms his nationality: spare features grown rather hawkish, piercingly blue eyes, a stiff upper lip with a clipped moustache which I don't remember, an affirmative mouth which I do, set in a straight mathematical line. He looks just like a colonialist come home from the backwoods: to stern, inflation-proof, redoubtable England.

In the evenings he avoids the promenaders from the hotels, who are a constant risk.

From the time the sun starts to dip the locals take to congregating in their familiar haunts: inside the less photogenic tavernas where the tourists don't venture, or under trees, or on balconies.

He is between the two worlds then. The English might see, they might chance to remember: he still looks too different from the natives and in his daily rounds he has kept too wary a distance from them for too long to be admitted by them.

So he stays at home. There are no houses closer than a hundred yards to inflict their noise and smells on him. Goats in a field rattle their bells, every once in a while during a long evening a motorcycle will phut-phut along a cart-track, blowing up a balloon of dust behind it. The leaves of the olive trees clatter tinnily, sounding as if they're made of some beaten metal; you imagine you can hear the glitter of the past in them, ancient armies marshalling.

He keeps indoors, or – if the night is especially warm – he sits out on his loggia. The setting sun is a great blood orange, sometimes the sky is green and septic-looking. Who knows what's going through his head then? Maybe nothing more than the costing of this month's budget – or speculating how he might make something from the lemons that fall from his dozen or so trees, into the long grass to perish to mush there.

I doubt if he has very ample means. He might be living (as I once did) with the rich, graceful, elevating company of oyster-shell and laburnum veneer and kingwood and coromandel marquetry, but at the same time be financially burdened: especially islanded as he is in the Mediterranean, in his Prospero's cell that is a confinement twice over – a thick-walled cottage and, in winter, what must seem to be a bleak, storm-bound outpost of the world.

Now they are dead and I am the only one left. Sometimes I feel I am no one, I feel akin to nothing so much as one of those

Javanese shadow puppets propped up on display in a dusty shop window in Bloomsbury which I pass daily, on my way to hunt things out in the British Museum Reading Room, under the whispering dome.

The justification for history is usually this, that if you know where you're coming from, then maybe – maybe – you will know better where you're going to. But history is an elusive and mysterious business; it is not some light-filled room where facts exist hard-edged. It's anything but: it's a shadow-show: it's patchwork, it's guesswork.

One morning I came close enough to him to engineer a collision. I did my dodgem bump as I intended and his wicker shopper went tumbling out of his hands. I saw as he rescued it from the road that he couldn't steady his hands, his balance was shaky. I noticed too that his cuffs were frayed: there was little of the dandy left about him now – except the straw hat. Its brim prevented me seeing the consternation that must have been showing on his face.

'I'm so sorry!' I said. 'Please excuse me!'

The English voice – and the necessity of courtesy to a woman, even such a clumsy one – momentarily trapped him. He was starting to say something, then he remembered. I heard no more than 'It's quite . . .'

I took a step or two backwards. From the rake of his panama I could tell he was keeping his eyes trained very low. At my espadrilles. But there was nothing there for him to recognize.

I let him past. He tipped the brow of his hat. He moved off, (I thought) shambling. We might have been strangers, with nothing in common between us except the location and this moment in time.

I stood there for a while longer, by the side of the road. He was hurrying downhill, at a kind of trot, into the blueness of shadows where the buildings meet at a cross and the church walls blaze white.

And that, as events turned out, was that.

I returned to my hotel.

I sat out on my balcony and smoked a cigarette and watched the sea. Twenty or thirty years ago, it occurred to me, the spot must have been blissfully quiet: it would have seemed like a kind of Eden then.

I picked up a copy of *Zorba the Greek* I'd bought from the stand in the hotel shop and which I'd already started to read. Digesting another couple of dozen pages, I realized better that Edens are really only confections we wish on nature. Crete in the book – or, rather, its people – sounded cruel and barbaric, and the more so the longer I read: a sly, possessive, jealous race.

I read on, till lunch time, letting the incident of mid-morning recede a little from my thoughts. I came to some sentences in the book which brought me up short: I read them and re-read them; a compulsion made me want to commit the words to memory.

I applied myself to writing . . . in the same way that savages in their caves engraved with a pointed stone or painted in red and white the famished and ferocious beasts who prowled around them. They too endeavoured, by engraving and painting these beasts, to fix them fast on the rock. If they had not done so, the beasts would have leapt upon them.

An idea came into my mind: it rested there over lunch, and in the course of the afternoon grew and grew. For days it grew.

When I wrote down in my notepad 'Sometimes I feel I am no one', even the writing of it faintly cheered me. It was something achieved, a point scored. On the melodramatic side perhaps, but that is as true and valid a quality as any other in life.

Who should have known that better than the person who held the pen – I, myself?

*　　*　　*

15

My father told me once, in a rare moment of confidence, that he and my mother had met each other at the Festival of Britain.

I learned no more of what happened. I'd ask about it, but it was as if he regretted having told me the first time.

When I imagine it now, there's little charity in my vision of the event. Charity and forgiveness from a child are privileges a parent has to set out to earn. It's too late now, for them and for me, when the damage is done and done for life.

I believe this, that each was probably seeking the other – a wife, a husband: and really it could have been anyone within the approximate range of their wants who might have chanced to fit that bill.

1951. Pea-soupers in London and crawling traffic and echoing klaxons. There was a hangover of secrecy from the time of the War. The days were murky grey, and food tasted of wood, but my parents were modern, 'expectant' people. They expected better than they had.

The 'New Age' was making shiny promises, and now after the years of winning a war and then stinting and scraping, everyone supposed they had the right to 'a better life'. My mother with her Saint Paul's School graces wanted to save herself from penury and from a vicarage life with her father in a Dorset backwater. Most probably my father, one of the 'new men' recruited to Whitehall, wanted to save himself from some nagging, bothersome sprite in his nature – an intuition which told him he might not love women, or might not love anyone; or he may have been alarmed that a bachelor's life was going to exempt him from promotion, or that the kudos of Cambridge and a double first didn't cancel out Surbiton and a grammar school for a background – he wouldn't be able to cover his tracks, he would tumble out of bed after a dream and find he was back there where he'd started.

They met that day, he told me – and, like angels, they dined out splendidly afterwards at the Ritz Hotel. I can picture them: my mother quite at her ease, perhaps waving to someone she recognized among the pink and white marble, my father less comfortable but wooed by my mother's performance and by the atmosphere, by the spectacle in mirrors of how they looked together.

In 1951, on sunny days or at dusk in the heavenly gilt dining room of the Ritz, far enough now from Surbiton or Dorset, the future must have seemed to them to glitter.

*   *   *

In reports of my father's disappearance, which I read much later, no one takes account of that, out of what it grew. They call him a 'traitor' because he 'betrayed his country's trust'. They claim the secrets he sold were not major ones, they relegate his crime to the second page, in among the advertisements. They sneer.

He was as true to his time as they. It was a crime of self-deception he was guilty of, as they said. But he was everything that made him, just as the newspaper writers took account of the accumulated hysteria of their readers. Just as they damned him in the lurid language that was expected of them, he too had done what he believed he needed to do and what those times, the 1960s, required of him.

What the newspapers couldn't forgive was that he betrayed Queen and country for what appeared to be so little, for such a miserable potage – for money, which was to be traded for the attributes of the good life. If he'd had a crack-brained dream of a flat or a dacha somewhere east of that infamous Iron Curtain, they could have ridiculed him and gone digging deeper into his past. But it was for nothing so pathetic and misguided: he did it for a Harrods account, for a self-contained house in a Kensington square and a second, week-end house on the windy Suffolk coast which we rented, then bought. He did it because marriage can become its own madness and love is a desperate fiction for those who are incapable of it, and because ambition and money seemed to be the simple alchemy by which England's

'New Elizabethans' were to be made.

The newspapers overlooked such matters, spiteful because it was only a chance motoring accident in the back of beyond and the man's thoughtless panic in the days afterwards which made an eventual exposé possible.

2

I don't know how to begin. After all it's my life I'm giving to you. Why and how I became the person I am.

I could start with my mother and father quarrelling through the wall in their bedroom in any of the hotels we found ourselves in that particular winter – till the manager of wherever it was requested us to please find alternative accommodation.

There were I don't know how many hotels. But time enough for that later.

* * *

Start again. In 1963 I was ten. My mother picked my name 'Annoele' ('Ann' + 'Noele') because she'd read it in a book and it had stuck in her pretty head. She never saw the embarrassment it gave me. She never really saw anything, though, except what she wanted to. At least my father knew how 'Annoele' pricked me when she said it – so he called me by my name as seldom as possible, he didn't call me anything at all if he could help it.

It had been decided that my mother and I would meet my father in Prague, where he worked, and then the three of us would drive back to London together: that was all I knew of the arrangements. But as my mother kept reminding me on the interminable train journey east across Europe, the plans were going wrong, things had been against us all the way.

'Mummy,' I asked her again when we'd crossed the Czech

border, 'when *will* we get to Prague?'

She was in her suffering Saint Joan mood.

'You've asked me that a dozen times. I don't know. Can't you see, I'm trying to read?'

'Will Daddy meet us?' I asked more cautiously.

'I told you – why don't you listen, Annoele? – he's coming to the hotel.'

She closed her eyes against the blue light in our compartment, against the snow – me – what was to come.

'I hate station sentiment anyway,' she said, more to herself than to me. She sounded languid, tipsy. 'Although I'm sure your father would manage to control himself. He's not very . . . demonstrative.'

She put down her bruised hardback of *Thunderball* with its torn cover and topped up her tumbler from the Chivas Regal bottle.

'All that snow, and no ice for this.'

She took a mouthful and swallowed.

'God in heaven, what's the point?'

How could I have known something like that? I sat on my berth, watching her and not caring if my anxiety for her showed.

'What's it doing now? Tell me, I can't bear to look.'

I eased up the blind and peered out.

'The train's going into it,' I told her. 'I think it's a blizzard.'

'That's *all* we need . . .'

Suddenly the carriage shook and she let out a scream.

'What's that?'

The wheels were juddering underneath us. I toppled back on to the seat.

'We must be *crazy*!' she shouted, with no one else there but me to hear.

In the next few minutes we ploughed into that blizzard. The carriage lurched – too many times to count – and we were flung backwards and forwards and sideways, all ways.

At a certain point the wheels couldn't cope any longer and

they seized up. We heard the engine groan and felt it slither to a halt.

It was happening in the middle of nowhere.

A quarter of the whisky in the bottle disappeared during the first hour we were stationary. My mother tried to read; then, slurring her words, she began again on her litany of complaints about everything that had gone wrong since we'd left London.

Behind the blind, I patiently sat rubbing at the condensation on the window, picking out cottage lights from the stars. Then the snow got so thick I wasn't able to see anything.

In all we were stuck there for thirty-two hours.

After just a couple of hours of it my mother erupted, yelling at the guards, who couldn't do very much anyway. She said it was outrageous, they didn't care what happened to us. (I don't think they had particular feelings really, which isn't quite the same thing.) They were so polite, in halting English and sign language. That should have shamed my mother, but she went on blaming everybody she could think of. Even me, because she knew I wanted to sleep and she said I was more selfish than anyone.

'It's insane! They don't care! We could die here! They just don't care!'

She began blaming my father. I'd heard it all before, a hundred times, a thousand times. I turned my head against the seat back so one ear at least was covered.

She settled some time in the afternoon, because eventually I did manage to sleep.

It was the next morning before the wheels were unfrozen, by giant acetylene torches unloaded from trucks. They roared like bonfires and spluttered sparks on to the snow. My mother had me fasten down the blinds completely when the noise and glare reached our carriage. She snatched up her *Thunderball* and said I would have to watch from outside if I wanted to, in the corridor, though God only knew why anyone in their right mind should be interested . . .

I left her in our cabin and went out and stood in a line with other people. I pressed my face against the cold glass to see. I listened to the dizzy wash of voices and made out Czech and German words and other languages – maybe Magyar, Rumanian, Russian – I couldn't recognize. I wondered to myself how it is we ever manage to make any sense at all out of the hot wind our lungs bellow up. It seemed odd too that I could feel I was one of them, these other people, and yet when I had a language in common with my mother I still didn't know the words, the simplest words, which would reach even a couple of feet between us.

*   *   *

My father came home from his postings every five or six months. There was no great fuss of preparation in the house beforehand. Only a lot of strenuous drawer-sliding in and out went on in my mother's bedroom as things were rearranged and presents he hadn't seen were put away.

Very little of his time was actually spent in the house. Most evenings I would sit in the nursery with Armand and Michaela Denis or Hiram Holliday flickering away in the corner, listening to the activity beneath me. Torrents of hot water raged down the pipes, the doors in the fitted wardrobe concertina'd open and shut as my mother's outfit was first settled on and then thought better of and exchanged for something else. The tallboy drawers slammed non-stop. My mother would be humming to herself, jingles from television advertisements.

I always watched them leave, through the banister rails. (Sometimes, after all their effort in anticipation, next morning would bring a rewarding mention in the William Hickey column; or I'd recognize them in a tiny box photograph in the *Tatler* and find the names *Mr and Mrs S.R.W. Tomlinson* in the fretwork of small print.) They looked like swashbucklers as they set out, glamorous pirates. My father wore a dinner jacket with a red cummerbund. My mother would be in her war paint: blue mascara, eye-liner so that her eyes shone in her face, a glow on her cheeks like the dead when they're dressed, magenta lips. She would follow my father downstairs, lifting the great bell of whichever dress she'd chosen: the heavy silver one with no back, or the black one she wore with long black lace gloves, or the full emerald gown with the fine white gossamer tracery on the bodice, or the favourite short scarlet cocktail dress with the sculpted breast pieces when there was to be modern dancing. (These dresses, it often crossed my mind, must be costing us a fortune. Or costing my father a fortune. 'If he's silly enough to buy me them, then that's *his* look-out,' my mother had told me once in his absence, but she hadn't said it again. To look so beautiful, though – I would manage to reconvince myself every time – what could the expense of it possibly matter?)

When they'd gone I would unfold myself from my crouching post on the landing and return to the blinking eye in the corner of the blue-lit nursery. It might be 'Armchair Theatre' or 'The Flintstones' that was on. The news which used to be of Korea was always about Algeria now, between the commercial breaks for Roses-grow-on-trees ('ooh!') and the White Tornado. I couldn't concentrate on the screen, I was thinking of my parents; I imagined them as two buccaneers, swinging from halyards into first-floor drawing rooms, jumping window-ledge to window-ledge to reach their next appointment, laying low the opposition with sabre smiles and cutlass conversation.

* * *

Prague, after our journey there, was a spate of mishaps.

When we'd found a taxi to take us to the hotel we were told by the man at the desk that our rooms were let. My mother wouldn't have anything to do with him, however, and seated herself regally on a chair in the hall and insisted she be allowed to speak to the manager. 'In person.'

The under-manager was summoned, and appeared. He was wearing a pin-striped suit and smelt of eau-de-Cologne. He replied most politely to each of the complaints, in French. My mother looked confused for once and pulled up the collar of her sable coat and sat snapping the catch of her best Asprey bag an alarming number of times till she seemed to decide that standing was the best procedure in such circumstances. (It wasn't the first occasion I'd heard her engage in a foyer wrangle.) She still wasn't going to permit it, she told him in deliberate English: unscrupulous persons in her position *might* have used their husband's diplomatic credentials, et cetera et cetera.

The under-manager had retreated behind his desk and was smiling very drily, pushing some letters round the counter with his manicured fingers. My mother kept her hand on my head all the time she was talking, towering over me.

* * *

Five days before we set out for Prague I'd sat on a green leather chair like a dentist's in Harrods' basement while a barber cut my hair and my mother loomed in the corner of my eye where she stood watching us both.

'Christmas time is party time!' the little man said, more to her than to me.

'For the children,' he added.

He looked just like an elf, with his jug ears and his spry darting movements as he snipped.

'Made out your note, your list of pressies? Sent it up the chimney yet?'

Each time he spoke he offered a formal bow of the head which he must have thought would endear him to us.

'You've got to look nice,' he said, his own face on a level with mine. 'Haven't you?'

Snip-snip and a bow.

'Pretty girl like you, shouldn't be difficult.'

He had such an oily smile, it filled the mirror.

'Christmas is my favourite time of the year,' he said – and bowed again.

'Oh,' my mother announced grandly from her vantage point where she could look down on us both, '*we*'ll be out of the country.'

'Indeed, Mrs Tomlinson?' he said, and looked up at her.

'Yes, we're going to Czechoslovakia.'

'Never!'

The scissors stopped cutting.

'Where our fairy tales started, you know. Annoele will be able to see the castle where Good King Wenceslas looked out and saw the old man gathering up his winter fuel.'

'Fancy that now!' The barber shook his head. 'Are you looking forward to it, going so far, Annoele?' The scissors snip-snipped busily. 'Yes, I'm *sure* you are, aren't you?'

I couldn't have smiled. I didn't, and just nodded.

'Well, you wouldn't guess it, would you?' my mother said.

I knew we weren't very far from a showdown.

'I don't think she realizes just how lucky she is, my daughter.'

I looked among the lotions.

'You *are* being a sourpuss, Annoele! Buck up!'

She was speaking loudly enough for the other mothers to hear, but she didn't seem worried about that, not today.

'Don't you *want* to go, for heaven's sake?'

'Yes.'

'Well, don't be a sourpuss, then!'

(Experience told me 'sourpuss' was one of the warning signals of worse to come.)

'You'd think you couldn't care less. Anyone else would be thrilled to go.'

The tiny barber, snip-snipping, didn't know which of us he should be siding with.

'*I* would be *very* excited!' he said. 'Going on a long journey like that. Travel . . . they say it broadens the mind, don't they? How lucky you are!'

My mother, I thought, she doesn't even see it's the barber's Christmas time too and all he wants is a half-crown tip instead of a shilling.

My mother felt so charitable that afternoon she gave him five shillings and then later said 'no' to me in Bendicks when I courageously asked if I could have a spiced tea-cake. It wasn't my place to ask, she told me grimly, making me feel I really was spoilt.

In Bendicks she didn't even want to look at me and blew smoke rings across the table and turned round to see the other women behind us. I knew it wasn't because she couldn't afford to buy everyone in the room a buttered bun — she always paraded her affluence: she was wearing her Canadian mink shopping coat and a small olive green velvet beret and new black Rayne shoes — it was only because I was her daughter and my thoughts or wants weren't allowed to matter.

*   *   *

On the other side of Europe, in the draught from the revolving door, I discovered nothing had really changed.

The under-manager had offered us accommodation on a different floor of the hotel but my mother was demanding we be given our original suite of rooms. I had to stand between them in my Loden-cloth coat and fawn top-stockings and leaky red shoes.

The man smiled at me nervously, and I tried to look impassive. I made my eyes like stones. My mother talked about 'Annoele' as if she was speaking about someone else not present. I was so tired I wanted to cry. I imagined marble knights and their ladies in English churches instead, and I kept my back straight as a rod.

We both watched as the under-manager consulted the register again. He spoke an aside to someone in Czech and I felt my mother's nails digging into my scalp. There was more delay — it was like a game — but in the end he did relent.

My mother snapped her bag shut for the last time, then she followed the man into a room – and left me standing. It happened so often like this: once my usefulness in a situation was over, she could just forget about me.

'How silly!' I thought as I always thought, and my heart filled as it always filled with a mysterious surfeit of pity for her.

I walked across to one of the windows to wait.

I watched the traffic, what there was of it. I wished I'd brought my 'I-Spy Cars' with me, so I could have been scoring points.

I recognized the makes from my *Observer's Book of Automobiles*, which I knew by heart. It was easy, anyway, with so few of them. The only cars on the streets in those days were Skodas and little Zaporogets and a few Moskvitches and Volgas and the Mercedes and Citroen embassy cars – and the heavy black Tatras from the government offices. (In the oddly caring and chillingly distant letters my father would write to us both, like a schoolboy writing to parents he hardly knew – did my mother ever read them, I sometimes wondered – he told us he was occasionally chauffeured about in a Tatra when his own unofficial maroon Jaguar wasn't deemed 'seemly' enough.)

I amused myself pulling the net curtain back whenever one of them rumbled past, skidding on the snow. I thought they were the ugliest cars I'd ever seen: like beached baby whales. They were all black, with an oval dummy grill at the front like a snarl and either three or four headlamps, inefficient slow-motion windscreen wipers which gave them a helpless look, and at the back of the older models, above the rear engine, two tiny windows like eyes or blow-holes.

After a few minutes I began to tire of Tatra-spotting and I watched the pedestrians instead as they negotiated the pavements of packed snow. It struck me that in London the streets would have been churned to slush a few days before Christmas. Here on Národní třída the shoppers hardy enough to brave the cold wore rubber overshoes and fur hats and reached out for

27

walls and window sills to keep their balance.

I couldn't decide what I felt more for them as I stood looking: pity – pity again – or a peculiar kind of envy for their unthinkingness.

*   *   *

Every evening in the house in Monmouth Square I ate my tea with the people of Algeria.

On the screen in the nursery I saw a few seconds of another person's misery everywhere the camera turned. A woman wailing over a bloody bundle in the street. A French soldier with a leg shot off learning to walk again on crutches. An informer with his mouth sewn up. Children begging pennies from the cameraman, scratching at the television glass. A lorry which had been loaded with survivors and their sticks of furniture upended in a ditch.

Inge, our Danish au pair, didn't censor my viewing. She attended to the pictures very straightforwardly and unsentimentally. Sometimes I looked at her to take my cue, to see how I should be reacting. Every evening when I wasn't being paraded downstairs for my mother's friends she watched with me, always in the same way, with the same disarming blankness.

I wished we could eat somewhere else, but it suited my mother best like this when my father wasn't at home. Often Inge was summoned to help her when she was getting ready to go out, and then supper had to be got out of the way first. I was still given my nursery fodder, although most of the girls in my class ate at the same table as their parents and exactly the same food would be served to both. I sometimes felt I was being fed like this so I would be kept young, like news pictures I'd seen on 'Tonight' of veal-calves with tubes rammed down their throats being force-fed with milk to preserve the richness of their meat, or French geese, with their webbed feet nailed to boards, swollen and unable to stand with the weight of food dropped into their balloon stomachs.

This was cruelty too; never mind animal rights – what about a child's?

* * *

I was remembered again when the luggage was brought into the foyer. My mother came back and I thought she looked ashamed of her inquisitive daughter standing in a little puddle of melted snow.

I was taken up separately in the lift with our big trunk and my mother's vanity case. I realized as soon as the cage's gates were folded back that the accommodation my father was providing us with was very superior, even by our standards. Porters jumped to attention, the lift-boy directed me forward with his white gloves, maids watched from the shadows. It must be costing the earth, I thought worriedly, stepping out on to the red runner and seeing through open double doors into our suite. (Whenever I cautiously mentioned *that* subject at home, to do with the expense of the evening dresses or of anything else, my mother would inform me it was none of 'our' business. As if how my father chose to dispose of his earnings couldn't matter to us, so long as we were comfortable. And he was always spending on us, always – even from far-away Prague – so that my mother would want for nothing and there wasn't any material convenience the two of us did not have.)

From outside in the corridor I smelt a log fire burning in our sitting room. When I passed through the lobby and angled my head round the edge of the door I saw my mother warming her hands at it. She was still wearing her sable coat, and she was looking at herself in the fancy gilt mirror above the fireplace: looking so intently that she didn't even notice me at first.

Tea arrived and my mother asked for another tray and had the waiter lay it and take it through to my room. She didn't need to say now when I wasn't wanted – our life together with my father so far away gave us an ironic telepathy at times – and I meekly collected my case and followed the waiter into my dark, stuffy cupboard of a bedroom, which looked down into the well in the middle of the building.

My bedroom was a disappointment after the other rooms. Everything else in our suite appeared to be so elegant: it suited my mother perfectly – or the image of herself she gave to other people, accoutred in her sable coat with her cream jersey dress underneath and the jewellery she'd brought on this journey, which would appear unexplained at home in scarlet plush Kutchinsky boxes on her dressing table.

When I went back through after my tea, pretending I'd forgotten something, I saw she didn't need me any more here than she did in London. She was still examining herself in the mirror, touching her face and turning it in the white light like a connoisseur picking over rare porcelain. I didn't feel resentment even, for my mother was beautiful. *She* knew it too, but how could I have blamed her for that . . .?

I just smiled. She stopped when she noticed me: yet it was scarcely a pause at all as she looked away and tilted her face higher. I stood in the doorway, enchanted. I didn't care what she thought of me, what hurt she might be wanting to do to me.

*   *   *

I knew what my condition was. I was dumbstruck – the way she'd intended me to be when we'd decorated the Christmas tree at home, just before we left.

That episode had left me cold, the whole exercise – setting the tree up and dressing it – it had refused to mean anything, even when she fitted the plug into the socket and the current looped through the yards of cable lights and two hundred little white candles flickered to life.

I'd been watching her face when she did it and she couldn't understand that.

'What are you looking at?' she asked me. 'For heaven's sake . . .'

'I . . . I . . .' I stuttered.

'What's wrong with you?'

She looked at me as if I must be possessed.

'What's wrong with you, Annoele? For God's s— . . . I've done all this for *you*.'

She mimed me gawping.

'I just can't make any sense of you. Sometimes you're not like a child at all. I could have been out, I didn't have to be doing all this. Did I?'

I didn't know the answer, yes or no, it was like the 'yes-no' quiz on 'Take Your Pick' when Michael Miles teased the competitors to make a mistake and lose the game.

'Well, *did* I?'

The one thought in my head was, is she so pale and angry because really – the strangest thought to have – she's *frightened* of me?

'There's masses I could be doing at Christmas time, let me tell you. Not that *you* seem to care . . .'

Then the telephone rang, making her jump. I followed her with my eyes as she went marching off to answer it.

I heard her speaking – not the words, but the laughing, up-in-the-air voice – and I just stood where she'd left me.

I blinked at the white candles and tried to be impressed and inspired by the tree, which I guessed was what she'd meant to happen. But it was difficult for me. It was difficult when I didn't know what to *believe*.

I peered among the branches at the parcels of shiny gold and silver paper, crossed and bowed with red ribbon. My mother had bought them made-up from the Christmas Decorations department in Harrods: they weren't gifts at all, but empty boxes inside which weighed hardly anything and were hung up gift-wrapped to make the tree pretty for whoever would see it. Anyone who saw would also think our generosity at Christmas time knew no bounds . . .

I heard the tinkle as the receiver was replaced on the telephone. I knew my mother would be checking her appearance in the hall mirror, smiling over the words from her caller: she might be patting down her hair – her auburn hair William Hickey mentioned every time – or licking lipstick from her teeth or wetting her little finger and smoothing her eyebrows.

My crime this afternoon had been watching her face and not attending to the thing she'd spent so long arranging for the final moment, the tree. She'd looked so beautiful in the festal half-light with the hall smelling thickly of pine, I'd only wanted to stand stock still and gaze at her. I'd been thinking, yes, now at last I can forgive you everything you do every other day of the year to make me wish sometimes you were dead . . .

Coming back into the hall, her heels rang on the black and white tiles. She saw me busying around the tree and her face darkened.

'What are you doing here?'

'I'm looking at the tree.'

'You were trying to hear what I was saying. You were snooping.'

'I wasn't, I wasn't!'

(I *had* been interested to discover – everything my mother did had a precious mystery for me – but I knew better than to try it that way.)

'Now you're telling lies!'

'I'm not. I'm –'

'Why can't you be –' the vexation was cracking her voice – 'why can't you be *normal*?'

In the troubled silence afterwards one of the cables failed. It was the last straw for her.

'Frig this tree! Just *frig* it!'

She stamped her foot. As a child younger than I would, I thought.

'I've had enough of this, I've had as much as I can take. I'm going out.'

She pushed past me. 'Inge!' she shouted.

She turned back and saw me feasting my eyes on her.

'Tell Inge –'

She lost track momentarily, seeing me transfixed.

'Tell Inge — tell her she has to stay in your room. Till you write a letter to your father.'

'What — what do I have to write about?'

' "What do I have to write about?" ' She mimicked me. 'The *tree*, of course! For God's sake, Annoele!'

She pulled the plug out by the flex and threw it across the floor. All the little candles died.

'I want to see that letter done when I get back, do you understand?'

I stood watching her in the kaleidoscope light made by the street lamp shining through the stained glass in the front door. I was fascinated by her anger, and quite at a loss to know how my doing nothing at all, my simply *being*, could cause such a fit of temper.

'Do you understand me? Answer me!'

'Yes.' My voice — I didn't recognize it, I didn't expect it to sound as it did — was quailing. 'Y-y-yes,' I said, nodding.

Even afterwards, confined to my room with Inge and both of us under strict instructions and the television voices still discussing the Kennedy business turned down low, I was excited just to watch her leave the house, gliding down the steps and out of the white portico wearing the ermine stole my father had sent her on her birthday and with a man I hadn't seen before waiting on the kerb to hand her into a low car. She had most dignity like this, when she was so angry and stern and cold with me (and probably wasn't thinking of me at all): when there were other people — hotel managers and under-managers, or my father's Foreign Office superiors, or our dinner guests, or her lovers — to impress. In Monmouth Square, glittering with frost, her throat shone with diamonds and the man brushed her shoulder with his fingers when the stole fell.

As she sometimes did, Inge circumspectly took a photograph from my window, which had the best view over the parapet, and I thought she did so for very wonderment.

Click — whirr — click, click.

Inge winked at me, which meant the photograph must be our secret.

I watched my mother in the car and I was open-mouthed, my heart thumped. She looked – there is no other word – bewitching.

*   *   *

Seeing her rapt in front of the mantel mirror in the sitting room of our suite, I remembered how the man had touched her just like this as the stole fell – appraisingly, like a collector, with the tips of his fingers.

The remembrance was so strong, from that and fifty other times I'd sat up to see her leave of an evening, I had the odd feeling that this new and latest geographical separation – Prague from London – which was meant to matter so much, counted for scarcely anything really. The difference was only a kind of accident. The buildings had wooden shutters, there were scenes from history and stars and bears and lions painted on the walls; I knew from books that the churches had onion domes like pepper pots and some were covered with gold leaf and shimmered for miles; I'd seen for myself that the people in the streets wore fur hats and rubber overshoes. Otherwise, the feeling told me, we hadn't moved at all. Or if we were moving, it was in directions that had nothing to do with specific places. (Now I understand better what it was: a journey without any maps, through the bleak freezing heart of one of the coldest winters in Eastern Europe for a decade.)

I closed the doors on the gold-and-white splendour and my mother like a temptress in the mirror. Behind her I had just a glimpse through to a second room with a round dining table prepared with a white cloth and three high-backed French chairs and wall-lamps with white silk shades.

I took care to let the double doors close together noiselessly. Above my head in the hallway I noticed there were glass panels set in the ceiling; daylight had almost gone, what little seeped

34

in was greenish under the crush of snow. It was a queer, unreal light.

The door of their bedroom was open as I passed. I stopped to look in, but went no further than the door jamb. I saw the bed where my father would sleep with my mother when he arrived with his things from the embassy apartment he shared: it had a huge sculpted headboard, gilded like the furniture in the sitting room. There was a chandelier, with some of its bulbs lit and the little glass chips spinning and chiming in a draught. The dressing table had a gilt mirror with three oval frames, and I noticed my mother's Vuitton vanity case was already half-unpacked. The creamy curtains were tied back with lime-coloured bows. There was a white fitted carpet instead of rugs. I thought it was a sumptuous room, what I could take in of it.

Walking on, I saw some of the bathroom too, next door to it: white and emerald tiles chequered all the way up to the ceiling, white mats on a green marble floor and a white bath like a ship with three gilt taps. The whole suite, I thought, it was like a palace for my mother: a white and coldly green snow palace.

My own bedroom when I returned to it was like a servant's by comparison. A radiator burbled and hissed in the corner. The narrow bed had a prim wicker headboard. The washbasin was small and unaccommodating. When I stood on a chair to see myself in the wall mirror, the wavy glass and the harsh glare from the strip light with the razor socket made me look slight and pale, so unlike my mother and how I imagined myself to be, drawing on a heredity of her fine looks – her racehorse profile, grey hooded eyes, arched eyebrows, thin lips, long sculpted neck, her auburn hair which she hadn't passed on to me either. All I saw was how bleary-eyed I'd got with so much tiredness.

I pulled the cord on the strip-light and stepped down off the chair. I quickly undressed in the last of daylight and climbed into bed without brushing my teeth. The sheets were like ice. I watched Saint Vitus's spires through the window as the cold sun sank behind them and kindled the sky pink. On this winter's evening the roofs of Prague made a furnace-blaze, all the distance I could see.

I shut my eyes and then I slept: the soundest, deepest sleep after our journey, for when I woke up several hours later I had the sensation I had sunk to the sea's bottom. The candlewick bedspread made me think I was lying on ribbed sand, my hands waved in front of my eyes like starfish. I had a strange dream in my head I couldn't account for – someone else's surely, or one I could only have learned in another element – of nuns stepping barefoot through a silent snowbound city where every building had a saint's or a martyr's name and, above the nuns' heads, white doves frozen stiff in the act of rising.

*   *   *

There were two kinds of social 'evening' at Monmouth Square. Either my mother was 'At Home', when she received her friends for drinks: or a proper, full-blown black-tie dinner party was staged, which entailed plans being made days in advance, sometimes weeks. It hardly mattered to me which my mother settled on: I dreaded the two sorts equally.

My orders for them both were the same: between a quarter past six and half past seven I was to keep upstairs and attend to my homework (this would be done to the accompaniment of either boozy chatter or roaring pipes as Inge filled my mother's bath) after which my obligatory appearance was timed for (on cocktail evenings) last drinks or (on formal nights) aperitifs before dinner. It must have been my mother's reckoning that on the dot of ten to eight, when I opened the drawing room door, guests could be counted on to be at their least critical and most forgiving.

Struggling at my school work, before Inge returned upstairs to get me ready, the answers always came to me slowly and with great difficulty. I would be thinking of the ordeal of performance that was ahead of me, when I would have to smile, shake hands, appear intelligent (being my father's child too). While my mother with her captivating looks swept all before her, taking the evening just leaning on a door pillar listening to a man's conversation, in a dress by Hardy Amies or from the Balmain shop, which would be cut to fit her as tightly as a sheath.

On dinner party nights – which had become the commoner kind latterly – when I was back upstairs again in the nursery I would sit up late, above the tidal ebb and swell of voices. I luxuriated in a cosy, toe-curling contentment then, with my duties over and hearing voices and laughter sounding up and down stairs and knowing I was forgotten about. Either I read (I liked E. Nesbit, her stories of the Bastable children who discover how precarious is their genteel life in the Victorian suburbs – 'Father was very ill after Mother died; and while he was ill his business-partner went to Spain – and there was never much money afterwards, I don't know why. Then the servants left and there was only one, a General . . .' – and the 'Railway Children' with an absent father unjustly convicted, who are smuggled into the countryside to escape the shame). Or, if I didn't read, I did what was easier and turned on the blinking eye in the corner.

I would switch the light off and huddle over the gas fire to watch. My favourite nights were when the house was especially full and no one had cause to be thinking anything about me and when the flock paper on the nursery walls ran blue and from out of the speaker on the brown and cream television set zither music played. In rubble-strewn Vienna the big Prater Wheel turned and in that shadowland of spies, traitors and self-deceivers Michael Rennie glided down a cobbled street in lamplight and became the foxy face and confidential, cheating voice of Harry Lime.

*   *   *

I woke hearing voices in another room and I realized my father must have arrived. My curtains were still drawn back and I saw lights across the city, so I knew it couldn't be morning yet. I'd pulled the sheet back and was pivoting my legs round to get up when something made me stop.

I couldn't hear what it was they were saying: only the tone. I remembered it from other times I'd tried to forget about – usually when they thought I wouldn't hear, when I played in the garden at home and the french windows were left open, or when I pretended to be asleep in the car, or worst, when we used to go to our white clapboard cottage on the front at Aldeburgh and I'd call up from the shingle beach while one of them ought to have been watching for me and no arm waves would come back, only angry voices blown with the gulls' cries and the shingle roar. It was much more restrained now, befitting the surroundings. I could only hear the pain in their voices, not the sense. My father's disbelief that nothing had changed; my mother needing to defend herself again.

I lay quite still, as flat as I could make myself on the cold sheets. I listened to the breath coming out of me and bells chiming the quarters across the city; I listened, counting down the minutes to striking.

On the hour I heard them, how I'd read it happened, the clockwork Christ and apostles making their passage under the sun and moon on the Old Town Hall clock.

I raised myself slightly and swivelled my eyes. The moon was silvering the cupolas and attic catwalks like a dream, the view was quite spectacular. Even so, at that moment I suddenly had a conviction – an omen, a tightening in my stomach – that Prague and what was to follow promised to be not the same as all our other holidays: it was going to be more fraught, if that were possible; those catwalks were crossed with trip wires, we must all be sadder in the end. (How could I have known that just by hearing the pealing of bells – without a third eye seeing?)

I had a tearful reunion with my father in the morning. He was standing by one of the windows in our sitting room, looking out. He started when he heard the timid turning of the door's handle.

'Good morning, good morning, good morning!' he called across, sounding full of brio and good cheer.

I ran over to him.

He made a circle of his arms.

'Are you glad to see me?'

He lifted me up. His clear blue eyes searched into mine.

'*Are* you?'

He was only ever like this for the first few moments on the first day after a particularly long absence.

'I do believe . . . you're *crying*, Annoele!'

It seemed to me just the sort of remark a father was expected to say. Fathers in television plays always spoke like that, it wasn't how he *felt*.

My mouth trembled. A smile broke on his taut, handsome face – as regular as the models' in the line drawings in the Chester Barrie advertisements, which always made me think of him – a smile that I should be moved to such foolish extremes for his sake.

Very clumsily he carried me across to the table in the second room behind the sitting room, not realizing I was too old for that now. My new Viyella lace-edged nightdress my mother had bought me in Woolland's was becoming rucked just under my bottom and I blushed at the worse awkwardness of my weight, but once he'd begun he must have thought he couldn't put me down. He slowly lowered me on to one of the high-backed chairs.

'Here. Look, Annoele. They've given us candied grapes. For Christmas. Grapes with sugar snow. We *must* be special.'

The crystal bowl sat in the middle of the table. Its cargo, even so early in the day, looked delicious and inviting.

'Which colour would you like? Which colour? Red or green?'

I managed to smile. 'I don't know.'

'You don't know? To pick red or green?'

'I don't know,' I said shyly.

'Why not?'

'I can't choose.' I shook my head. 'It doesn't matter.'

'But it *does* matter,' he said. 'You must. You *must* choose.'

'I don't mind.'

I considered which I wanted more.

'Red,' I said, with no particular reason.

'You want some red grapes?'

Then, just as impulsively, I changed my mind.

'No. No, green.'

My father laughed to see me so perplexed.

'Well, then,' he said, 'if you can't decide –'

And he took the bowl away for punishment, out of my reach, still laughing. I sat waiting, expecting him to bring it back, but he didn't, not then or later: and there, uncommented on, it stayed all through breakfast – at the other end of the table, too far for me to stretch out my arm.

My mother was smiling when she came into the dining room, and involved with me, interested.

'Good morning, Laura,' my father said.

She walked past the remark.

'Good morning, Annoele. Did you sleep well? Have you got a nice room?'

It passed, though, her show of concern, like winter sun on a wall.

'I asked them for tea, not coffee. Ring the bell, Annoele darling, will you? I do *not* drink coffee for breakfast, I should have thought that was simple enough to remember. It's a filthy *foreign* habit –'

She sat on the chair with the highest back and surveyed the contents of the table.

'I thought it couldn't get any worse than that train. Thirty-two hours late, hardly an apology, we have to fight for a taxi at the station, we get here and they tell us the rooms have been re-let. *Very* sorry, smiles and bows. That, I said, is not how *I* view the situation.'

'You have to be patient here.'

'I beg your pardon,' she said. Her voice was as sharp as a lemon. '*I* don't *have* to be anything.'

'There's a Czech proverb. "Patience brings roses." '

'Thank you, Harry Wheatcroft. Please spare us the folklore.'

I giggled, with nerves as much as anything else. My mother flashed me a look.

'May I remind you,' she told my father as she unfolded her napkin, 'roses do *not* bloom in winter. Even you with your degree of knowledge about gardening should know that.'

'The countrywoman speaks . . .'

Her mouth tightened.

'Virginia Woolf –' my father began, 'she wrote about roses bloom–'

'Virginia Woolf isn't of the remotest interest to me, thank you very much. I want my breakfast.' Her voice started to rise. 'I want my tea. I want white bread, not these –' she dropped some on the table '– bloody rolls.'

The door opened and the waiter walked in, carrying a tray.

'I presume,' my mother said, amplifying her voice, 'we *are* bugged? The newspapers say so. They eavesdrop everywhere. I expect they'd almost given up on us . . .'

There was another hiccup in the service. My mother did not care for Ceylon tea, which was being suggested.

'I should like some China tea,' she told the waiter fortissimo.

He looked confused. My father said a few words to him in Czech and he nodded. Their exchange must have reminded my mother – if she really needed reminding – that here she was in an utterly foreign land.

After that, when the waiter had gone, she bridled: in just a few seconds she became frosty and aloof. My father tried to bring her down out of it, but she wasn't going to come. She'd been a Dorset vicar's daughter when my father married her and now she was a chatelaine. (Probably too – even then I suspected it – she was sown with the seed of my grandfather's embarrassing 'illness': now we never visited him or discussed him – although things like mental imbalance are comparative.)

'They don't seem to care if they understand their visitors or not.'

She was looking daggers, and made me think of the Eskimo woman in Harrods.

'Is that one of their quaint customs here?'

She aimed her words at the back of the door the waiter had just closed behind him.

'I don't know how you stand it,' she said. 'It's the sticks here.'

'You'd get used to it,' my father told her. 'Really, you would. In no time.' He smiled. 'I just wish –'

'We've had this discussion how many times –'

'We could have dinner with the others. They're –'

'They're *your* life.'

Her eyes turned vindictively on my father.

'They have nothing to do with me. We decided all that. If you'd meant me to spend my life trailing round Europe after you, you should have told me at the beginning.'

It was my mother's turn to smile: a smile of such ghastly cold reasonableness.

'I did *not* come all this way to discuss it again,' she said.

I was wishing I was back in my bed, with the sheets pulled up over my head: anywhere but in the same room as the two of them.

My father was paling.

'I'm not sure why you *have* come,' he said simply.

'I thought it would be educational for Annoele.' My mother's eyes seemed to be accusing me. 'I thought *she* might enjoy it.'

I saw they were both looking at me. I set my eyes like marbles and stared at the cover.

'I did it . . . I did it as a gesture of good faith,' she said in her mysterious, other-worldly voice she hardly ever used with my

42

father. The words sounded as if they'd been memorized from somewhere, from a book or a television play. I glanced up again and intercepted a look being exchanged between them: one of some adult knowledge not meant for me.

'It's Christmas time,' the soft voice continued. 'Isn't that good reason enough?'

She tipped her cuffs back. One hand reached up to smooth the auburn hair that turned heads, which always looked glazed and basted and like a meringue.

'What's that?' my father asked.

'What's what?'

He was peering. 'On your wrist.'

'This?' She lowered her arm. 'It's a bracelet.'

My father watched keenly as she turned it with her other hand. It might have been the most innocent gesture – or she might have been trying to conceal it.

'I don't remember it,' he told her.

She hesitated fractionally. 'No. No, you haven't seen it. That's why.'

'Is it new?'

'New-*ish*.'

'This year? Last year?'

'Last year, if you must know.'

'Where did you get it?'

There was a single second's delay before she answered.

'Kutchinsky,' she said.

Had she forgotten he hadn't seen it? Was wearing it a mistake, an oversight? Or was it deliberately meant as a provocation to him – a goad?

'I bought it,' she said.

'You *bought* it?'

'Well . . .'

My father seemed to be thinking, considering.

'*I* would have bought it for you,' he said.

She looked at him: not with gratitude, but with a smile that might have been disdainful.

'You weren't there to buy it for me.'

'No. I –'

'I needed it *then*.' She turned her wrist. 'I saw it, I liked it.'

(My head was echoing. *You're lying, you're lying . . .*)

'You only needed to say.' My father was almost breathless, he seemed absurdly moved by such a little thing. 'You only –'

'Well . . .' My mother tilted her wrist, letting the bracelet catch the light. 'I have it now.' It hung heavily and solidly. 'It wasn't *so* expensive.'

'That doesn't matter. You know that.'

I looked at my mother's face and thought I caught – could it possibly have been? – after the disdain, a fleeting expression like *remorse*.

My father stared at the bracelet gift I'd seen her wear for her guests a dozen times. Then the door opened, and his eyes looked up as the waiter spoke.

I don't exactly know what happened in this next interlude, with the waiter there. There was no new quarrel, no flashpoint, but I sensed the crisis coming at any moment. The temperature seemed to dip, the room was colder; I began shivering in my nightgown. With a fourth party for an audience, my mother became very sneering, dropping butter plates and jam dishes about the table and complaining non-stop.

They should have realized at that point and had us put out of the hotel as soon as they were able to. Their first presentiment, even before our arrival, had been the right one. But maybe difficult customers are a welcome challenge after the anaemic run-of-the-mill clientele who simply pay up and never seek to question?

The waiter retired with my mother throwing a roll after him and hitting the door, telling him that in France (whatever France had to do with it) she only ate warmed bread at breakfast time. It wasn't the truth, of course, but I didn't say anything for our shared appearance's sake. I was remembering her father telling me once, when we still visited him, that I should always think the best of other people and be charitable.

(What I conveniently forgot that morning was my mother's response, her icy reply to him that charity was supposed to begin at home and her pushing me out of the room in that smelly, tumbledown thatched vicarage.)

*   *   *

The Christmas before, 1962. We were in a restaurant, my mother and I, to meet yet another man: but 'discreetly' (always 'discreetly'). This one wasn't young; he had a cigar wedged between his sharp dog's teeth.

There was a tree in the centre of the smoky room, reaching up into the skylight in the ceiling. Long thin strips of shredded tinsel hung down from the branches and the effect whenever a draught blew from the door was like falling, dripping water. The meal lasted for hours (it seemed) and all I could do was watch the tree and imagine I was diving, I was fathoms down.

'Stop staring, darling!' my mother told me.

Again she told me.

And a third time.

'Stop it!'

But I couldn't. It was no use her saying anything to me. Didn't she see that?

'Annoele! The wind will change!'

My mother was looking her best, which strangers seemed to bring out in her, strangers to me. Everything shone, she was working on current. I don't know all she must have taken beforehand to get through those occasions, laughing and simmering like a boiled pot for hours on end.

There and then I had a premonition – like the feeling I would experience in Prague about our holiday as I lay in bed watching the moonlit roofs – that this day was going to be different, not like the other ones at all.

Her foot stamped on mine under the table. I endured the slow, numbing pain of her sole pressing on my instep with all

45

the anger that was in her, till I persuaded myself I couldn't feel the torture any more.

'Annoele, she's very like her father!'

The man nodded. My mother wouldn't explain further. I saw the pointed bulbs in the trees like translucent, hovering fish.

I said it, when I did, slowly.

'You're . . . you're standing on my foot.'

I didn't care that the man had to hear too.

My mother tried to look surprised.

'*No*, I'm not!'

She smiled desperately.

'Yes, you *are*,' I said.

Very, very gradually the pressure eased. I reached an arm under the table and took off my shoe to rub some feeling back into my foot.

'She's very pretty.' The man spoke round the Havana in his mouth. 'Is her father good-looking?'

My mother's eyes were on the cloth. She spoke quietly. 'I don't want to discuss him.'

'It all comes from you, does it, Laura?' The man laughed.

My mother stared at him, discomposed by that laugh.

'What would Annoele like for Christmas?' the man asked, turning to look at me. (He's asking me, I realized, to save our lunch and to save the day.)

'I don't mind,' I said.

'You don't mind?' he repeated me. 'Well, that's easy enough! Some husband's going to be delighted to catch you one day. Isn't he?'

He guffawed again.

'I don't want to get married.' I pronounced my words very clearly, so that I wouldn't be misheard.

'Oh? You don't?' He rolled his eyes at me. '*You*'ve got high principles, haven't you? Do these come from your father too?'

My mother looked imploringly at the man in the silence.

'Don't –'

'Come on, Laura, it's only fun!'

I was determined I wasn't going to answer him, not ever.

Then suddenly, out of sheer frustration, my mother turned on me.

'Why do you have to be so . . . so *awkward*?'

'I'm not,' I said quite coolly.

'Don't tell me what you are,' she snapped back at me. 'I said you're awkward.'

'You said I should come.'

She smiled – at the man, not at me – a terrible smile of no hope left.

'I thought you'd enjoy seeing a lovely restaurant, that was all. Thousands of girls your age would give their eye teeth to be having lunch here. Never mind all those starving children in India.'

She looked across at the man, who was watching me with his eyes screwed up.

'But not *you*, of course!'

She couldn't help saying it, although it must ruin our lunch and their day.

I watched my mother as she began to cry, into her pink napkin.

'I can't . . . I can't . . .'

'Annoele . . .' – the man leaned forward to say it, breathing smoke into my face, '. . . hop off to the Ladies', will you? Your mother –' he touched her arm '– I want to have a few words with her. Here's a pound, two pounds. No, take this five. How's that? Buy yourself some chocolates, at the desk. A box of them.'

He was grinning, but it occurred to me he was doing it anxiously, and only because there were other people there to see us.

'See what you want, eh? Good girl!'

I took his money and pushed my chair back. The pianist tinkled at the glass piano; the room thrummed with politesse.

I was wrecking their day – but, if this was a victory, it wasn't giving me the elation I'd imagined. As I walked away my eyes seemed to be very far back in my head, shrunken and hard. From the door I looked over my shoulder and stared at the two of them as they sat at the table consoling each other. I could feel no satisfaction at what I'd done.

What kept me from enjoying it? Was it the shock of seeing the dog-man's tenderness? Was it knowing that I'd taken from my mother her glow? Did I remotely perceive what I understand now: that her physical beauty was a mystical quality in our lives, and that by wanting to make it appear any *less* than it was I was only impoverishing all of us who depended on it?

*   *   *

I think my mother felt she'd never had anything she'd been due, not even a mother: no sisters, no brothers – and maybe that was where it all began and brought her back to? Perhaps subconsciously she was wishing the same fate on me?

But that's speculating in ways I'm not qualified to do. All I *can* say is that, whatever the reasons were, my mother needed me to suffer – not bruises and weals, not at all, but social discomposure: the disgrace of being associated with her when she made a scene in public and people were watching us. Perhaps too she knew I had the pride in her that made the hurt to our dignity seem much worse, so that when I tried to imagine her behaviour was turning me into another kind of person, metal-hard and invulnerable, I felt inside my old self I was really betraying her, I was rejecting her.

I sat with a ramrod back, staring at my breakfast cup of milk and my saucer as the squeaky trolley wheels faded away out of hearing down the outside corridor.

My father sighed wearily, crossing his hands on the table, and my mother indignantly told him he didn't need to sulk, why hadn't he said something to back her up in front of the waiter? She called him 'hopeless' and a 'coward'. It was too much for my father and, before I was ready for it, he brought his hand crashing down on the table.

'For Christ's sake! Can't you bloody think of anyone else but yourself?'

She could match him in that mood and a long slanging match began. I sat opposite them, too frightened to say anything, to move a finger, a muscle. They accused each other of selfishness, and I knew in my heart of hearts — where these sorts of truth are supposed to live — that it was exactly the case. I didn't have the words at the time, but I appreciated the situation by a horrible, precocious instinct: I had parents who'd given each other a child as a gift, a propitiation, a kind of talisman to protect their privacy, which was what they really loved best in the end — my mother smarter than a cover girl with her secret evenings in the West End when she left the house, my elegant, sombre father in Prague with his work and (for relaxation) his dilettante's love of history — and when they were obliged to meet I would be shuffled between them like a parcel neither of them wanted to have the final claim on.

*   *   *

Seven candles on a cake.

'Happy birthday, Annoele!'
'Happy birthday, Annoele!'
Click.
Whirr.
Click. Click.

— I'll take one of her holding a slice of the cake.
— Who says? Anthony Armstrong-Jones? We *are* honoured.
— Please, Laura, you're in the way.
— I'm in the way, am I?
— Can you cut her a piece of the cake?
— Whatever happened to 'please?' Don't we use it now? Has it gone out of fashion?
— Please, Laura!

49

— Please what?

— Can you cut her a piece of the cake? For my photograph. *Please*, Laura!

— 'Please, Laura!' 'Please, Laura!' No, I will *not* cut her a piece of the cake.

— I'm trying –

— I can't, it's got candles on it.

— Can't we blow them out now? *She* can blow them out.

— Well, wouldn't that be pretty?

— Please . . .

— She has to make a wish first.

— Yes, a wish! Did you hear that, lovely birthday girl across the table?

— God in heaven . . .

— Mummy says you have to make a wish before you blow the candles out. Have you got a wish? What's your special wish going to be?

— Annoele's wish? Oh, I can tell you that. Don't you know? She wishes – don't you, Annoele darling? – she wishes that *we*'d never got married –

— Laura!

— . . . and she wishes *she*'d never been born.

— For God's sake!

— Not when Annoele can hear, I know, don't tell me!

— I think you've –

— – drunk enough? Look, just don't tell me!

— Would you cut her a piece of the cake? For my picture. For *my* sake. *Please*!

— No. I can't, I said.

— Well, *I*'ll have to do it.

— Leave that bloody cake alone. It's got candles on it.

— I'll blow them out, then.

— Don't touch them!

— For my picture . . .

— Sod your picture!

— This is rid—

— Just sod it! *I* bought the cake, *I* lit the candles. Get that into your head, will you.

— It's her *birthday* . . .

— And who forgot it was her birthday? Look, you're not blowing those candles out for *any* effing picture.

— She can *hear* you, Laura!

— I don't care. I'm not cutting it. I'll cut it when the candles are done. And when *I* like.

— Please, put the knife down.

— Won't this make a picture for you too, then?

— Put it down. Come on, put the knife down.

— Well, we *are* going at the father figure bit, aren't we? Later's better than never, is that it?

— Don't, for God's . . .

— She can hear? Yes, she *can* hear. Look, let me tell you something, Mister Simon Tomlinson. We're warping her. Every second's a little death to her. She'll never forget this, what we're doing to her.

— Laura! Please, please!

— She won't forgive *me* and she won't forgive *you*. That's all I want with *my* wish. So she'll never think *you* were right and *I* was wrong.

— She doesn't think any such –

— Yes, she does.

— You're just –

— I'm not anything. Don't tell me what *I* am, what *you* think. I'm sick of it, all so bloody right and I'm wrong every time. Just screw your bloody cake! Look!

— Laura!

— Come on, how many slices? Bloody, pissing slices. There! Now your picture's on the wall, Anthony Armstrong-Jones!

The cake flew round the room – on to the curtains, the ceiling, it was trampled into the Persian rug. The tablecloth caught fire; and the man who came to repair the table's mahogany wasn't able to correct all the damage, the deep knife slashes as well as the scorch burns. The room with its serene Regency proportions recovered its physical appearance eventually – no expense was spared on the task – but what did that matter set against the violent truth of those lives it held?

*　　*　　*

I forget every single thing that happened that particular day, but even then I was conscious I was remembering what seemed to be the important parts; I was saving them up.

I was taken out twice to see Prague – firstly by my father, in the morning, and then when he grew tired of me and after much bargaining, by my mother. (She wanted to go to a concert in the evening – to give her a change of surroundings, I suppose – but all too clearly she didn't want me there as well: so a couple of hours of my company in the afternoon was settled between them as the exchange.)

My father took me walking in a park first of all, which was always the sort of unimaginative thing he did, which he thought fathers were expected to do. I tried to get closer to him then, this sallowly good-looking man with the chiselled Chester Barrie profile whom I hardly ever saw: I did try, but his leather gloves and my striped woollen mittens were making the kind of closeness I needed impossible.

I smiled to him instead – sweetly and coyly, how my mother did to her men friends when they each came calling to take her out of an evening. He made an effort in the snow and the cold to put as cheerful a face on our life as *he* could. We smiled, and other people smiled at us as they hurried to their work or made for the queues outside the food shops. Some children laughed and shouted in their language and threw friendly snowballs at a dog. While what I was feeling was that glass window between them and me and between my father and myself that I'd pressed my face against on the train. I was sad about it – beyond my years – but I didn't want my father to see and I martyred myself to keep smiling. I smiled at everything, and perhaps my father thought I was deranged, like my mother's father: always smiling, at the children running after the dog, at frozen players on a bandstand pumping out oompah-pah-pah music, at the keen clear blue of the sky.

We just kept walking. As his duty my father took me to the sights or, if they were too far, he showed me where they lay. He took photographs of me, lots of photographs.

'Watch the steeple, Annoele!'

Click – whirr – click, click.

'Just look natural, now – be yourself!'

We saw all we could cram into a morning: the black-faced Virgin in the Holy House, the hog's-back lanes of rusty-tiled roofs in the dilapidated Nový Svet (the 'New World'), the bright green copper cupola of Saint Nicholas's, the sprawling faceless Černín Palace (which was the Ministry of Foreign Affairs, he told me), the queer little house in a back street where Beethoven once lived, the faded fresco of the Last Judgement in Saint Vitus's Cathedral, a cold and grimy place and like walking into the darkness of a whale's inside. I was photographed against them all.

And then later – later – what matters, we're standing on hard-packed snow on a modern bridge. I'm dead on my feet but also exhilarated and extraordinarily clear-headed. We're watching barges passing in the middle of a wide river. The river is the smoky green colour of jade, not bleakly grey like the Thames. Bits of ice float in it, carried down from the snow-lands I saw from the train. I move as close to my father as I can, I stand beside him while he points things out to me. I feel for his fingers, I want so much his comfort, a word or look on his face (always so diplomatically blank, so professionally noncommittal) that will tell me this moment together – so together – means something different from all the others.

I took his hand, I thought he gave it to me.

'Where did you meet Mummy?' I asked, launching in, surprising myself that now I felt I could ask. I'd always speculated, but I'd never dared put the question at home, so near where it must have happened.

' "Where?" ' He looked at me, equally confounded. 'That's an odd question to ask, isn't it?'

He didn't say it unkindly, as my mother would have said it.

'Was it – was it an accident?'

His brow crinkled, and he seemed to be considering.

'Yes,' he answered the question at last, in his deliberating voice. 'Yes, I suppose it was. A kind of – "accident".'

We walked on, side by side, in silence.

'Why do you want to know *that*?' he asked.

I mumbled. 'I don't know.'

'It's history now,' he said. 'It's a long time ago.'

I scissor-strode in time with him. He seemed to have sunk back into his thoughts.

'Can you –?' I asked.

' "Can I –?" '

'Tell me?'

He started flailing his other arm. Then he slowly filled his lungs with the thin, heady air.

'*Well* . . .'

He said it very slowly. It was as if he was taking time to decide, should he tell me or not.

'Please,' I said.

I didn't know why I was so anxious to hear.

His face shone with the intake of oxygen. I could see he was warming to a revelation.

'You're so interested to know?'

'Yes,' I answered.

'Well . . .'

'You've said that,' I reminded him. 'What's after that –?'

'I'll start again,' he said.

He took more breaths.

'Before you were born . . .' he said – beginning the way Inge always used to begin her stories in the nursery – ' . . . a couple of years before you were born, in nineteen fifty-one, there was a lot of ballyhoo.'

He paused.

'Why was that?' I asked him, to coax him forward.

' "*Why?*" '

'What for?'

'Well . . .' He lifted his shoulders. 'Everyone was supposed to be very . . . patriotic.'

'What does that mean?' I was almost certain I knew, but not quite.

'It means being proud of the country where you live, where you're born.'

'Oh.'

'Something was supposed to be happening, you see.'

'What?' I asked.

'I'm not sure. I wasn't sure *then*, really. Something "in the air". A new "mood", the newspapers called it.'

'Didn't anyone know?'

'The government did. Or they pretended they did. The message got a bit lost, though. "Scrambled", we used to say.'

I nodded, to encourage him.

He hesitated. I realized it wasn't an easy thing for him to explain.

'You see, after the War,' he began, 'it was very dull in Britain. It was still rations. Grey days. And secrecy, from the War time. "Keep it under your hat" – have you heard of that? "Be like dad – keep mum", "Telling a friend may mean telling the enemy". Murky days. Pea-soupers in London, days when the traffic crawled and all you saw were their headlights. Tooting their horns. There was never enough of anything, you never got what you wanted, or even what you were meant to make do with instead. Food tasted like wood. It was very vexing. People thought they deserved better. So they did. It wasn't what they'd expected would happen.'

He paused.

'Wasn't it?' I prompted him.

'We'd won the War. The Second. There were still bits of the Empire left – the red patches on the atlas.'

For one confused moment the word 'red' made me think of

Russia. It was only for a moment, though.

'The Commonwealth?' I said to him – but he didn't seem to hear me saying it.

'It was as if, too, people'd had some of the stuffing knocked out of them.'

I nodded again. There was another pause, our legs slowed. I had the feeling he was really talking as much to explain it to himself as to me.

'Everyone just muddling around,' he said. 'London was a dismal place, you've no idea. In France the government bought over the bombed sites in towns and started building on them again. In Britain no one could make up their minds what to do with the destruction – and they did nothing.'

'What happened?'

' "What happened?" ' he repeated.

'In stories things always happen.'

'Well, we were told something *would* happen. But it was very vague. Somehow everything would . . . come together again. Things would be exciting. Britain was going to be very forward, very modern. "Progressive" was the word. That meant lots of bright new ideas.'

'Was that what happened?'

I didn't know if he'd heard me. He seemed to have his own train of thoughts to pursue, to find words for. Again I saw he wasn't talking just to enlighten *me*.

'There was a big celebration – called the Festival of Britain. They built the Festival Hall for it, beside the Thames, where so many streets were bombed and gutted. It was a fine building to raise out of all that: white Purbeck stone –'

'Purbeck? Where the fossils are?'

'White stone and walls of glass.'

'Like a phoenix?' I suggested, remembering the legend from school.

' "Like a phoenix?" Yes. Only – when you looked out the windows, out of all that glass, you were seeing just the same London.'

'The bombed places?'

He nodded.

'There were fireworks shows and concerts and exhibitions to go to – new inventions to look at – things made in factories up and down the land. It was very impressive.'

'I wish I'd seen it.'

'But it really only lasted while you were there, that atmosphere. You just had to look about you: all along the South Bank. The buildings the bombs had missed were left standing, like tombstones. There was so much rubble. That was London too.'

We'd stopped. He stood looking across at the elegant vistas of government palaces and avenues of leafless trees.

'And that's where we met,' he said.

I was following his eyes, to the quarter where he'd told me his apartment was – then I remembered.

'Where the bombs were?'

'Yes. At the Festival Hall. We'd gone to see the exhibition – separately.'

We turned back to the path and resumed our walk.

'How?' I asked him.

'We were each looking at a display, the same one. I think it was a stand of record players – or television sets. Radiograms, it might have been. We just started talking. Just like that.'

'What about?'

' "What about?" '

'What were you talking about?'

'Just the record players. Or television sets, or whatever they were. Radiograms. The room was full of new gadgets. Refrigerators – washing machines – cocktail cabinets – ciné cameras. That kind of thing. What everyone wished they could have.'

'What happened?'

'It took them a long time to get them . . .'

'No,' I said, 'with *you*. You and Mummy.'

'Oh. We just started talking. About what was there.'

57

He thought for a while, for as long as it took us to walk past – I counted carefully – seven of the evenly-spaced trees between us and the road: as if the time he was telling me about was as far off as history.

'We saw the rest of the building. Then we went outside. Along the Thames – we looked across to the Embankment.'

I counted four more trees.

'We found a taxi and we went off. To Piccadilly. We had dinner at the Ritz Hotel. In all that old-fashioned gilt and splendour.'

Five – six – seven.

'And your mother kept humming bits of a song – a nightingale singing, angels dining. Do you know the one? "There's magic abroad in the air." I really thought there was . . .'

He stood with his breath steaming in front of him. 'And . . .?' I wanted to ask him, but hadn't the courage left to speak.

It was then, at that point, he just changed the subject, quite suddenly. He was looking at the river, at the barges, when he began telling me, very patiently – in such a methodical-sounding voice – about the niceties of international law's rulings on river traffic.

That was all.

I let him talk as we continued walking, until his interest in the subject must have waned and he stopped in mid-sentence. He said nothing more after that: either about navigational procedure as decreed by courts of law or about his first meeting with the woman he would marry.

I could feel my hand going slack in his. Eventually he seemed to realize – and he let it go, gently. He smiled at me hesitantly, and we walked on.

I trailed my left hand along the embankment's frosty railings. I decided I wasn't going to let my tiredness show, not on any account.

Listening and looking down I could hear the ice cracking in the river – it sounded like cubes splitting against the sides of a tumbler, the chunky crystal kind my mother drank from when

58

she said she needed 'courage' – and I felt a lovely terror welling up inside me which I wanted to share with this man and knew in these seconds I never would.

*   *   *

In Florence one afternoon during the Easter of 1959, when my father was down in the hotel bar and my mother was soaking in the bath, the telephone rang in their bedroom.

I picked up the receiver. A man's voice, low and throaty, rumbled out of the earpiece. I let him speak. It was in no language I recognized.

I spoke at last, during a silence, feeling I was expected to. 'I think you have the wrong number,' I meant to say, but the line went dead before I could crank out all the words.

I forgot to mention it. My father was looking even more pensive than usual that day. My mother was still at the stage when she blithely pretended she could live with us both. Maybe it was the contrast between her giggly cheerfulness and my father's burden of thought that put the telephone call out of my mind.

My mother, refreshed after her bath and douched in perfume, was hectoring us to make the most of our time.

'Buck up, Buck Rogers!' she said to my father. 'Let's go out. There's no point staying inside, is there?'

He didn't respond.

'Is something up?'

'What?'

'Shake a leg!'

'I'm . . . I'm sorry.'

'So you should be!'

She was balanced on one heel, transferring her notecase and wallet of traveller's cheques and lira from one handbag to another.

'Well, I'm going to the shops. Stick if you want to. Are you ready, Annoele?' she called through to my room.

I was standing behind my door, observing them both through the crack.

'It'll be educational for her,' she said.

My father mumbled something, agreeing.

'Well, Simon, are you coming?'

In those days she could say his name and it didn't sound like a curse.

'*You* go,' he told her.

'Aren't you feeling well?'

Instantly her voice had a metallic ring.

'Yes. Yes, I'm fine.'

'Maybe you don't want to be seen with me? Is that it?'

She laughed. Florence was too much her 'kind of place' to leave her out of sorts for long.

'Annoele!' she called through to me.

She tossed one of the bags on to the bed.

'At any rate,' she said, still smiling at her joke, 'we will disregard the insult, we shall soldier on regardless . . .'

That holiday, while we two shopped, my father spent much of each day at the window overlooking the Piazza Massimo d'Azeglio. Only a few photographs were taken as a record of that week – click, whirr, click-click – Annoele feeding pigeons/Annoele admiring the Duomo/Annoele expressionless on the Ponte Vecchio. Creative inspiration flagged in Florence: my father focused his Hasselblad on 'infinity', just to prove that we'd actually travelled there and we'd seen the sights.

When we weren't shopping or doing the obligatory tourist treks we stayed indoors, up in our rooms, out of the heat. I kept a careful watch on my father then. I had no pride in what I did, because every time I sneaked a look while feigning to be occupied with something else quite innocent I convinced myself I was committing a treacherous act. I would remember spies in television plays with cameras concealed behind their ties, and for the first time in my life I was troubled with guilt. But equally I couldn't seem to help my actions. I was intrigued, both by his silences and by the capacities for deceit I seemed to be uncovering in myself. It was no use my thinking – as I tried to – that it was a *different* Annoele who was watching him. I knew quite positively it was a betrayal each time I did it, homing in on him like the Hasselblad.

With all that close attention I missed nothing, even though I could make no sense of his behaviour. Florence *did* change him, outside and inside. In a week two creases had grown across his forehead and he'd learned how to make his mouth into a grim straight line. A few times the telephone rang and, carrying it into a corner of the little sitting room, he spoke another language into the mouthpiece.

Usually he just stood at the window above the piazza, keeping his post. I didn't know – and I still don't know – what the daily vigil meant: if it was really a signal to someone we couldn't see. All I knew was this, and it was bad news: he was hundreds and thousands of miles away from us, further than Vienna where he worked then, further than London, further than Surbiton in the mists of dead time.

Back home in the square in Kensington it would happen there too, the phone ringing our ex-directory number and a stranger's voice talking.

I'd hear my mother asking, very distinctly, who was this speaking to her please? The caller would always offer some excuse before the call was hastily terminated.

My mother would replace the receiver on the cradle, looking sombre and perplexed. It was never the time to disturb her, then.

*   *   *

In Prague my time with my mother in the afternoon was just as stilted as the morning with my father had turned out to be in the end.

I stood beside her in the hotel foyer while she fastened the buttons of her sable coat, then brazenly inspected herself in the mirrored walls of a display case.

'Where did your father take you?' she asked me.

'Miles.'

'Well, then,' she said, 'you've had your exercise for one day, haven't you?'

'We went to a park. And the Old Town. Daddy explained about it. We saw Beethoven's house. And old churches.'

'Lucky you!' she said – and I knew she didn't mean it. 'Did he tell you in Czech?'

'In *English*!'

'I'm surprised he remembers what to speak. They talk gobbledygook here. That's what it sounds like. A lot of turkeys.'

She licked some lipstick from her teeth.

'Do you . . . do you think he makes it up?'

'The language? Oh *no*!' I was quite shocked.

'What else did you do?'

' "What else –"?'

I thought about what we'd done.

'He talked to me a bit,' I said, intending my answer to be honest but diplomatic.

'Oh? He "talked", did he?' Now it was my mother's turn to sound surprised. 'Congratulations, Annoele! How on earth did you manage that?'

She shook out her silk square.

'What do you mean?' I asked her.

'Well . . . He's not a master conversationalist – a raconteur – is he, your father?'

I was puzzled how I should reply, I couldn't think. I stood watching her as she laid the scarf with the lightest touch on top of her coiffure.

'Well, well!' she said. 'Such loyalty, I must say!'

She pulled the knot of her headscarf tight under her chin.

'And what did you talk about?'

'Oh . . .' I pretended to be innocent. 'History.'

'*That*. . .!' She rolled her eyes to the ceiling. 'I don't suppose you got a word in edgeways, did you?'

'It's interesting –'

'It sounds fascinating!' She wrinkled her nose. 'You've had enough of museums, then?'

'It wasn't . . . wasn't just museums.'

She shot me a look in one of the mirrored angles in the display cases. I shifted my eyes, but not quickly enough. She must have seen my face reddening.

I took a few steps backwards. I studied the pattern of gondolas printed on the silk of the scarf.

My mother straightened up and stood coaxing her fingers into neat gloves like elegant hawking gauntlets: blue suede, expensive-looking, and smelling as if they were new and unused.

'He thinks too much of the past, your father,' she said tartly – and then she snatched my hand.

We set off at speed. Outside – down the salted steps – and, catching a break in the traffic, off across the boards set down on the snow for pedestrians.

On the opposite pavement we hurried towards the corner of the block. I saw a photograph of President Kennedy in a shop window, in a black frame.

'What are the shops like here?'

'I . . . I didn't notice,' I said. 'Not really. We were –'

'Oh, of course. You told me. You were both too busy "talking", weren't you?'

I looked back over my shoulder, to the hotel. My father was standing at the window of our dining room, watching the street.

When he spotted us, he went through the motions of looking interested. I waved timidly.

We turned the corner. Suddenly, out of his sight, my mother dropped speed, she slowed to an elegant amble.

'What about there?'

'Where?' I asked.

She straightened her collar and pointed ahead to a hood over a doorway.

'I'm so sorry it's not more cultural. But I'm thirsty, I'm tired, and Prague is getting on my nerves.'

I didn't know what to say.

'It's all right –' I began.

But she went walking on and didn't listen. Her arms wrapped round her waist, fitting the fur to the contours of her body.

A man lifted his hat to her and she breezed past him, not seeing.

'Annoele!' she called testily. 'Come on!'

I ran after her: afraid of her anger, of course, but jealous to protect her as well, to keep her just for my father and me.

It called itself the 'Orbis', and a notice in the vestibule translated into English said it had been a coffee house as far back as the turn of the century.

Inside, it was hot in the clammy way greenhouses are. We seated ourselves at a little marble-topped table in a corner, on a crimson plush banquette side-on to a window, and we immediately slipped our arms out of our coat sleeves.

I sat back very primly, I was unable to disguise my feelings about what we were doing: that it was wrong, it wasn't what my father had meant, sitting in cafés like this was too easy.

My mother noticed my disapproval, and she wrinkled her nose again and sniffed.

I turned away, to the window. I watched the people walking past on the street and looking in. They weren't like people in London, I thought, there was no envy and hardly any attention even on their faces.

I put my fingers on the pane of glass. I felt – I'm not sure why – it was like another frontier on my reading of the world.

I saw my mother's reflection in the window. She was looking past me, round the room, as if I was too young at ten years old to matter to her. I thought, it's like Bendicks, maybe she wants the customers at the other tables to presume we're strangers to one another?

Behind us an enormous oval mirror in the panelling, with gilt cherubs climbing up the frame, reflected our heads an infinite number of times off the window and all the mirrors on the other walls. I kept getting glimpses of us everywhere I looked in the room. It embarrassed me.

My mother had noticed the reflections too, but I could see they weren't troubling *her*. I watched her watching, adjusting the angle of her head, smoothing the plucked arcs of her eyebrows, patting her hair down so that it was like a nest. She appeared not displeased with the afternoon's images of herself. (But, I thought, how could she *not* have been made content and satisfied by how she looked?)

I sat beside her being especially quiet, knowing she was always worst with me when I interrupted her most private calculations.

One of the waiters came over and my mother gave our order in English, in a loud voice – a black coffee for herself and (she didn't consult me) a hot chocolate for me – and when they arrived we sat in silence sipping from our cups. When my mother had finished and was tired of searching for herself round the room, she examined her long bony fingers on the table. (She didn't have the kind of hands that are made for a domestic life, for everyday woman's work. I never thought of her as in any sense at all 'ordinary', I didn't want her to be, nor did my father. Physically she existed on a purer level than either of us or anyone else we knew. That in her – her fated aloneness because of how she looked – had always excited me.)

After an hour, or an hour and a quarter, it was time to go back to the hotel, and I thought she looked sorry to have to stir herself. I followed her following the maître across the room; we were like a little cavalcade or caravan. The customers' heads turned and we continued staring forwards. It was a performance really – my mother's mien of airy, chaste indifference; for that matter so was the maître's sycophancy a performance, and my bridesmaid dignity. Everyone must have presumed we had interesting, exotic lives; I supposed at the time that's what they must be thinking, it was why they were surrendering their own dignity, craning their necks round, to observe us both.

*　　*　　*

Another year.

Three people are descending from a train in the Stazione Santa Lucia in out-of-season Venice. It's been a long, long journey – the wagons-lits have French plates on them – and the trio is decidedly fractious. Not glaringly so, because they're British as an informed watcher could deduce from their muted clothes. Burberries and tweeds and flannels. The man has a tic in one steely eye, brought on by the journey's forced confinements. The woman's mouth is turned down. Caught between them, I – for the child of seven or eight years old is me – find it hard to suppress my relief at our arrival, gulping in the smoke of the other trains.

My father wasn't on his regular leave: he was en route between London and somewhere else, and we were making a short holiday of Venice. Later, in the hotel, he recognized a former colleague and his wife from the Oslo embassy.

'I don't believe it! Look, Laura!' He stayed her with a hand on her arm. 'The Haywards!'

'Who are the Haywards?' my mother asked coldly, moving forward out of his reach.

'Rex. And Diana. From Oslo. What a coincidence! Come on, we've got to –'

'We've got to nothing.' She nimbly anticipated another arm-hold and steered well clear. 'Please leave *me* out of it, if you don't mind.'

'They're great people! You'll –'

My mother lowered her voice. 'Maybe they *are* "great

people" — as you care to put it — but I have not, I have *not* come to Venice to join in a Foreign Office reunion.'

My father looked confused, quite at a loss. 'But you'll *like* them —'

She pivoted round on her heels to watch them and it seemed to me that as she stood there with her mackintosh open and her hands on her hips she was fastening on them the evil eye. (Why did she feel she was obliged to despise that couple, like everyone and everything that had to do with my father's work? Was it because she thought the life was futile, being a diplomat in a world where the American eagle and the Russian bear knew all of each other's secrets? Or was it because she realized that her experience and her character didn't equip her for the task of being a diplomat's wife? Was it because she was reminded, every time she was surprised by people like the Haywards, that the same life was the one we depended on ourselves, to live as graciously as we did — which my father had made our expectation in life — and so much more graciously than *them*? Did she see that there was a startling disparity between their situation and ours? Could it even have been that she actually *knew* about my father, or she had a glimmering at least, how much he was sacrificing for her sake, to turn us into 'New Britons'?)

My father tried encouraging her.

'They've always wanted to meet you.'

'Well, you can spare them that disappointment.'

'What do you mean?' My father stepped back to admire her. 'You look fine! Wonderful!'

But that wasn't what my mother meant, not at all.

For the length of our stay she continued to shun the couple, trailing me through the streets with her for company, into boutiques and cafés.

'Cafés,' she told me — as if now the Haywards in their plus-twos and walking brogues were quite forgotten and had no power to trap us — 'cafés are a form of civilized life the British have never encouraged.' That was the most meaningful history lesson I had on our short, unsatisfactory sojourn in that city of mirages.

The ocular difficulties began first thing in the morning, looking across the lagoon from my window and not seeing a horizon, only a sweeping continuity of milky blue. On our walks reflections wavered in the canals under buildings: or the *buildings* and not the reflections wavered, it might even have been. The sea light we walked in confused with its shrillness, showing solid objects upside down in water but also making you see an apple or a plate on a table or a lamp post in a square quite afresh, with the confidence of its three dimensions you'd never taken account of before. Then at other times the light softened and a view when my mother stopped long enough for us to look at it was like a run of watercolours on wet paper or it had the slurriness of a crayon sketch. Also, the salt air tired me, and I was too young for those distances, so everything shimmered doubly for me.

My father complained of a headache on one of the middle days. My mother turned to look at him with her eyes very small and shiny, and it seemed to me she didn't believe him.

'We'll leave you then,' she said, but not in a tender or understanding way.

We two dressed for the cold, and went out. It was a foggy afternoon, like a London one. Everywhere was lit, but dimly. My mother tried on shoes in a Gabrielli stockist, and then in Ferragamo. One pair she *quite* liked but wasn't sure about: at the last second, as the assistant was repacking them to return the box to the shelves, she cried out, 'No! I'll take them!' The box was wrapped in scarlet gift paper and gold ribbon and my mother nodded to the woman to hand it to me. I took it and the assistant smiled down at me. I looked up at my mother for a clue as to how I should be reacting, but she'd noticed a display of scarves and was concentrating hard on those.

Later, the shopping mood gone, we went into a grand café.

My mother asked me where I should like to sit. I chose an oyster-coloured banquette on the outside wall, next to a window. I laid the parcel with exaggerated care on the little marble-topped table. Two young women, identical twins dressed to the nines in matching fauntleroy velvet and lace, raised their eyes from the silent game of cards they were playing to consider us both: then dropped them again, to their hands.

My mother unwound her white angora muffler.

'Isn't this nice?'

Immediately she was thawing.

'I haven't been to Venice for – for so long.'

'When? When did you come?' I asked her. 'Did you come with Daddy?'

'Oh *no*.'

She said it with great emphasis.

'With grandfather?'

She was in a good enough mood today to smile, even at that.

'No, not with him.'

I held my hand out and she gave me the muffler to keep for her.

'With a girl at school. Marcia Young. And her family. Just after the War.'

She untied her headscarf.

'We were staying in Yugoslavia. On the bit of coast at the top. They'd been lent a house.'

I took the scarf from her: one with a Liberty pattern of peacock feathers.

'I came over. For the day.'

'Did you all come over?'

'No,' she said. 'Just me. With Marcia's brother.'

I neatly folded the scarf into a smaller square, then another.

'What was *his* name?' I asked.

I felt I wanted to know, very much: and that for once she was wanting to tell me, about her past which she had always kept so hidden from me. The fog outside and now the warmth indoors were bringing us together and such a thing couldn't be reasoned. The chance, I seemed to know, might never come to me again . . .

'Tom,' she told me. 'Tom Young.'

'Didn't your friend want to come?'

'Marcia? No. She said she'd been. She was the one who suggested it. Tom and I, she said, *we* were to go. We definitely *had* to go to Venice. She was quite insistent.'

'Tom Young' was a new name to me. I was imagining someone dark and rather dashing and devil-may-care: like my father to look at, but not so solemn as he sometimes was.

'What did you do?' I asked.

'We came here. Believe it or not.'

'*Here*?'

She scanned the room, slowly and hesitantly.

'I wasn't sure if I wanted to see it again. I'm glad now I've come.'

'Where did you sit?'

'I don't remember that. There was an orchestra then. It was quite cheap in those days, after the War. It had just been redecorated. I thought it was the most beautiful place I'd ever been to.'

'*Then* what did you do?'

' "*Do*?" '

'Did you dance?'

'No. No, not that.'

'Can you remember? What you did?'

'Well . . . We drank mocha. I remember that, because I'd never drunk it before. It sounded rather sinister, but it wasn't, not to taste. And . . . What else? Well, I remember Tom was very good company.'

'How?'

' "*How*?" I don't know. He was very . . . just very funny. Very – what's the word? – "*wry*".'

'He wasn't serious, then?'

' "Serious?" ' She looked at me, amused and puzzled. 'No.

70

Not at all.'

'Did he make you laugh?'

'Oh yes!' She smiled to remember and I thought how seldom she'd ever allowed herself to smile so naturally with me. 'He had me falling all over the place, Tom did.'

She eased her fingers out of one glove.

'But he was very considerate too. He showed me as much of Venice as he could, and told me all about it. He didn't make it sound at all . . . well, dull. That's how it *could* have sounded: all those doges and assassins they had. It was a very cruel city, Venice.'

' "Cruel"?'

'Yes. It was a very modern state, you see.' (Could this be my mother, who would usually speak as little as she could to me? Had Venice performed a sea-change – on her, on us both?) 'The people in government got rid of whoever didn't agree with them. Tom made it sound exciting. Even though it *was* history. I've forgotten it all now. That part.'

She unpeeled the other glove. She seemed to be trying to remember: the skin on her face tightened with concentration.

'We went in a gondola. I thought it was going to be very pricey.'

'Was it?'

'Oh, Tom wouldn't tell me. He wouldn't have told me something like that.'

'What else did you do?'

'He bought me some coral beads. Bits of coral, I mean, threaded together. And flowers – from a shop he rushed into – a bunch of yellow asters – which I had to carry around with me. I didn't mind *that*, though.'

She smiled again and examined her fanned fingers on the table top.

'I think people imagined we were on honeymoon. But I was still at school. It really was the strangest day.'

'Where is he now?' I asked, wanting us just to go on talking like this and not to have to stop, not for hours.

The smile disappeared.

'He died.'

' "He died"?' I repeated her.

'Yes. He was in the Air Force. It was an accident.'

She paused.

'I think it was, anyway. A kind of – "accident".'

There was another longer pause – then she continued, without my prompting.

'It happened in Holland. We were told he was given the wrong directions. Someone in London misread something. Or the message wasn't heard properly in the plane. It got – what's the word? – "scrambled".'

All the time I was thinking, why is she being so forthcoming? Her confidence was embarrassing me, as if I had no right to know, and it was also giving me an exquisite happiness: both those feelings together.

'He flew into a wood. It was kept secret "why". They said he was test-flying something new.'

'What was it?'

'I don't know. We never knew. They wouldn't give us the details.'

' "*They*"?'

'The War had made everyone so edgy,' she said, not seeming to hear me. 'Or maybe – maybe he was carrying something.'

'What was he carrying?'

'He flew on missions. "Damaging information" perhaps. I once heard someone say that. A bit of the past that had to be destroyed. Papers the government didn't want people to know existed. Whatever it was.'

She turned her attention to the menu. A waiter was crossing the room. In front of him my mother asked me what I should like and she seemed to be very concerned that this day I should have what I really wanted.

'You must tell me what you want, Annoele. Would you like hot chocolate? No? Not this time? What about tea? Yes? What kind of tea would you like? Jasmine? That has petals in it.'

Yes, I was saying to her, yes – yes.

'You're quite sure, now, that's what you want?'

She smiled entrancingly at the waiter, then gave our order – in pidgin English. He bowed, like a pantomime flunkey. Behind him the sisters dealt again and spread the cards in their hands.

I thought how much more relaxed my mother was looking just because she was away from the hotel. She hummed a tune very quietly under her breath: not the one about nightingales singing, angels dining, magic abroad in the air, which I was to learn about later, but another one I didn't recognize, perhaps from the day when she'd listened to the orchestra with Tom Young when he was still alive.

The sisters played from their hands. Figures in the square walked past the windows, women in hats and fur collars and men sporting scarves in the Italian manner, thrown over one shoulder.

Our tea when it came was hot and delicious. (Tea, not mocha, I noted.) Tiny blossom heads floated in the brew and I counted the number in my mother's cup compared with mine.

'Let's have a cake,' she said. 'Shall we?'

She told the waiter, and when he'd served us she halved it. Our elbows touched as we ate with our forks, and I couldn't help feeling it was like a treat, a women's treat, not having to share the table with my father, whose presence was becoming enough these days to make disturbing waves in a room if my mother also happened to be there.

Was it thinking that which caused me to see him? I turned from watching the expressionless faces of the sisters and his shape seemed to be crossing the square, with another man's. I was sure it was his London topcoat and Lock's hat: I thought I recognized his walk, the scissor-sharp stride his legs took, knees held stiffly. The other man was making movements with his arms, like directions.

I touched my mother's elbow and realized too late – something in that sudden, fierce intake of breath – that I

73

shouldn't have done so. The Italian *Vogue* she'd been reading lay open in her lap while she watched the disappearing figures. I heard steel heel tips clicking, how my father's did.

The fog was adrift in the square; the lamps on the other side were as remote and eerie as hazard warning-lights in the sea.

We waited a while before we got up and left, and then it was done in silence. My mother's good humour had passed. I felt that, unwittingly, I was somewhere close to the cause of it.

Outside she became impatient that I lagged.

'Come on, Annoele. Don't dawdle!'

'I'm not dawd –'

'Don't answer back! I've told you that a thousand times, haven't I?'

It wasn't for reasons of perversity that I did it, only because my legs couldn't keep up with hers or even with my own thoughts. But how could I tell her that?

Back at the hotel we came upon my father sitting in the front hall. His camel coat was draped over the back of the chair and his hands played with the hat. He seemed not to recognize us at first. He was pale and looked unwell. He smiled slowly at us – from so far away – from some other country. I saw him for the first time as a man who didn't belong to us – we didn't own him – he had another life that was apart from us.

My mother started, as if she too was discovering him, or she had forgotten, or she had not understood fully. She spared him a smile, but it was as cold as the afternoon.

My father spoke quietly, in a careful voice. He'd been out, he said: to get some air.

My mother's smile continued to chill. Standing a few feet away from them both, I felt I was only an observer, not their child.

'Yes. We saw you.'

My father looked surprised.

'Where?' he asked.

'We were having tea. You were walking across the square. Annoele saw you.'

He glanced at me.

'*She* pointed you out.'

I felt my face very hot. Holding the parcel of shoes I stared past my father, into the warren of little lamplit lounges.

'It was dark,' he said.

'Yes, it was.' My mother snapped the clasp of her handbag open and shut, open and shut: always a bad sign. 'Didn't you want to be seen, then?'

My father was watching my mother the way I saw other men do: with a kind of awe, a hopeless coveting. I dare say I was used to that look, even from my father – especially from him. I remember it now and I realize it was not the natural behaviour of a husband, what we accept as being 'natural' and 'normal'. It was disbelieving and afraid, and I can't doubt I also glimpsed pride shining through: the pride of possession.

My mother and I, we couldn't have understood what all this was costing him – the way we lived and we expected to live. The qualms to which I was prey came later. My mother may have been aware of more than she pretended: or perhaps she refused to let herself consider the matter, she disregarded it. I think she believed that marriage was a gamble – financial, emotional, and whatever else – and you merely grab what you can from it. She was mercenary – in money matters and all else too – and so she was more 'modern' than we could have conceived.

Now I am persuaded of the truth of this: that, so early on, *my father was selling his soul*. Or the business was beginning at least; the preliminary soundings-out, and such half-way houses as Venice and Florence and (another year) Lausanne were a perfect foil, as well as the disguise we permitted him. My mother – may it be said as a kindness of her – if she suspected as much, she simply did not want to know.

On the last night of our stay in Venice we hired an open-topped motor launch for a trip out to the Lido. It cost a bomb, of course; I think it was done for the noblest reasons, however – to leave something enduringly pleasant in my mind.

The sky was inky blue, not black, when we set out some time after eleven. The needle stuck on the maximum number of knots and it was a very, very fast ride. We sat on a bench at the back with our scarves blowing in our faces and spray spitting in our eyes. The isthmus of Lido didn't have very much for us to look at when we got there. A few lights twinkled through trees. It was a blustery night and the trees were thrashing their arms about. The big hotels were closed and the serried rows of chaises on the white sand looked silly and sad.

My father tried to smoke a cigar but it wouldn't keep alight. My mother repeatedly coughed into the back of her gloved hand till he understood her disapproval and flung the butt into the sea. At the last second, dropping from his hand, it threw out a little shower of sparks. He gave me a good loser's smile and shrugged his shoulders under his camel coat. My mother in the middle of the seat pulled the knot of her headscarf tighter against the wind and cold; she crossed her legs becomingly and slipped her arm under mine but, as the driver swung round and the spray flew, I noticed her face hardening for the chilly journey back, I saw the look of infinite grudging that was the thing that frightened me most about her now.

Four or five years later we did experiments at school with bottles of pressurized gas and were shown what happens when you unloose the top just a fraction; sitting in the lab in far-away St Neots, with rubber bungs exploding around me and ricocheting off the ceiling, it was a night in Venice I was thinking of.

*   *   *

Walking back up the steps into the hotel in Prague my mother grabbed my hand.

'If your father asks where you've been, you can tell him we went to a cathedral.'

76

'There he is!' I cried out and pointed.

He was sitting in the lounge nearest the foyer, reading a Czech newspaper which had a front-page photograph of Jacqueline Kennedy in mourning weeds. He was also smoking a cheroot.

My stomach contracted. My mother hated cheroots. She hated not being able to understand Czech even more and people concluding from that that she was an ignorant woman. (Her father, the eccentric clergyman, had stinted to send her to Saint Paul's: 'The best school in the King's realm' he'd called it from her childhood, not seeing any good reason to change his mind later, even when she had to be rusticated for a term for misconduct (undisclosed), and much later when he was certified by the medical authorities to have diminished responsibility for his actions.)

My mother looked haughtily at my father and pushed me in front of her as if she was returning me. My father guiltily stubbed out the cheroot in an ashtray and put the newspaper down.

'Did you have a nice time?' he asked us, with the strain showing on his face. 'Both of you?'

'Yes,' I said.

' "Yes, *thank you*," ' my mother corrected me.

'Yes, thank you.'

She sighed. 'Considering what's spent on your education . . .'

'She's on holiday,' my father said.

'Manners don't take a holiday.'

'Laura . . .'

She walked past him, to where she could see herself in one of the display-case mirrors.

'Annoele told me what an interesting chat you had this morning,' she said, removing her headscarf of gondolas and sweeping a hand over her hair. 'Talking about the past.'

My father stretched his lips in a dry smile.

'Did she?'

'What a pity I wasn't there. Give her a chance and Annoele is probably quite a little teller of tales.'

'Oh . . .?' my father began.

My mother was inspecting the calibre of clientele in the hall.

'I'm going upstairs to lie down,' she said. 'I'm exhausted. Did you get the concert tickets?'

'Yes. Yes, they're here.'

He showed her and she took them and found a corner for them in the hold of her bag, beneath another of her battered, weather-beaten books, *Diamonds are Forever*.

'We'd better not come up and disturb you – if you're lying down?' my father said. 'What will . . .?'

'What will you two do?' My mother's eyes passed over us, they hardly saw us, but still they managed to suggest some complicity was linking us both and she didn't trust either him or me. 'I haven't the faintest idea.'

She walked off and we watched her, my father and I. The lift gates slammed shut behind her.

I sat down on the chair next to my father's. There was a pause.

'Do – *do* you "tell tales"?' he asked with another cautious smile.

'No.' I shook my head and felt the tips of my ears burning. 'I write things down, that's all. In my diary. Mummy doesn't like it. It's not "telling".'

'Why do you do it?'

'It's just sometimes.'

'Will you write all this down too?'

I looked at my galoshes. 'I don't know,' I said despondently. 'I don't know if I want to, really –'

There was another pause, which I felt I was creating.

'You must be thirsty?' he asked.

'I . . .'

From my complexion he must have been aware that I'd been sitting in a hot room, not traipsing about in the cold. He tactfully referred to neither, however – the outing or the deception – and he clicked his fingers to summon a waiter.

'Would you like some milk? And a mille-feuilles to eat? There's a trolley of cakes. They have very good cakes here, sometimes I come in for one.'

He called across an order. Then he sat slumped in his chair, with his arms lying between his legs and his hands dangling. He looked far away in his thoughts. I wondered if he imagined that I really did tell tales.

We sat for a long time, waiting.

'Are you going to send some cards?' he asked me at last. He smiled again, and it seemed like a forgiving gesture. 'To your friends?'

'I keep forgetting it's Christmas.'

'You keep forgetting?'

The smile remained on his face. I realized he was trying to lighten the mood.

'Yes,' I said, and nodded. I smiled too, at the fact Christmas could slip from my mind.

'We'll have ours when we get home,' he said. 'You have to enjoy yourself, Annoele. Will you? – do that?'

His voice had a pleading note in it.

'It's a happy time,' he said.

I must have looked doubtful.

'Don't you believe me?' he asked.

'I don't know.'

'You'll get your presents when we're back home. You'll believe it then,' he told me. 'You'll have a happy Christmas then.'

I made another pause happen.

'Is Christmas always "happy"?' I asked. 'Why do we say "*Merry* Christmas"?'

'Well . . .' I watched him looking at the lines of time and fate on his palms, turning them over, lacing his fingers together. 'You'll be happy when you get your presents. You will be then, won't you? That's what Christmas is about. Giving and receiving.'

It was like earlier in the day, our walk by the river: as if he was saying things to confirm them for himself. He looked distracted, how he'd looked then. I thought he also seemed anxious now; his movements had a peculiar jerkiness, like his changes of expression.

'Exchanging gifts,' he said. 'Putting our presents under the Christmas tree. Asking for what you want and having it given to you.'

He stretched his mouth to another smile.

'I see,' I said.

To get us off the subject, I asked him which route we would be taking on our journey. He explained – with relief, I thought – and mapped it out with his finger on the table's glass top. Through Austria – to Salzburg – to Innsbruck in the Tyrol maybe – on to Zürich, or possibly to Munich if the Vier Jahreszeiten there had rooms – across France, by way of Lorraine – up to Paris – and then to Calais and the car ferry, arriving in London on the evening of Christmas Eve.

'Now, here's your milk,' he said at the end of it. 'And the trolley. Which pastry would you like, Annoele? Take your time.'

I didn't want them – either the milk or the pastry – and after I'd been served by the waiter I could hardly make any headway with them. It upset me I hadn't even been asked if I wanted them, and I was just as much irritated with myself that I hadn't said anything as the order was being given.

For quite another reason I was also *grateful* as I sat there trying my hardest to swallow what was in my mouth: for my father's sake, that my mother hadn't been there to see him clicking his fingers when he'd called over to the waiter. That was my only consolation of the afternoon. Sometimes my mother condemned everything he did as 'vulgar' and 'beneath' her, and it was as if they both gloried in the insults and put-downs, they were what the two of them wanted to believe of the other. (There were occasions when it seemed to me that our lives were endlessly complex: bluffs and double bluffs . . .)

I'll say that of my father, at least – in spite of my mother he persisted in being outwardly a gentleman: but then she wouldn't have married him if he hadn't been, so the case of his being anything else simply couldn't have arisen. (A proper society wedding might have come along for her, but he'd made his old-fashioned proposal when she believed she needed saving from her wandering, incontinent father in his Sturminster Newton vicarage whom she wouldn't let us visit: and my father in those days of despair in Dorset had suited her very nicely indeed.) She didn't seem to see, even a child can know the craziness of saying someone's such-and-such when he clearly isn't. In that respect she underestimated my intelligence very badly: she presumed that a child she'd done so much to harm wouldn't perceive any inconsistencies, any muddles in her thinking.

'Drink up your milk,' my father was encouraging me. 'Don't you want more of your cake?'

'I'm very full.'

'After your walk, aren't you hungry?'

'A bit –'

Did he see that my loyalties were divided?

'*M'sieur!*'

We both looked up at the word. The supercilious undermanager with the manicured hands was standing over us.

'*Téléphone, m'sieur. S'il vous plaît.*'

'Telephone?'

My father seemed perplexed.

'I'll be back,' he told me, getting to his feet. 'If you want anything more . . .'

'No,' I said and shook my head. 'No, thank you.'

He didn't smile as he nodded to the under-manager. His face was suddenly weary and drained.

While he was away I tackled the mille-feuilles again. It was sweet and rich, but I could have been chewing over ashes in my mouth. I thought, why was anything to do with us like the Croesus story in reverse? I began to persuade myself for the second time since we'd arrived in Prague that *being here* wasn't a special event in my life at all: glorious Prague with its saints and legends and wisdom, the lions and bears rampant, the zodiac codes turning on weather vanes and swinging from sign-hooks. Being 'here' or 'there' or anywhere in the world was just an accident of geography.

He came walking back, my father. He didn't seem to know quite where he was. He looked shocked, and dropped into his chair.

'Was it your office?' I asked him. 'On the phone?'

He stared at my tumbler of milk.

'What?'

'Was it your office?'

His eyes didn't move.

'Were they phoning you here?'

'No. No, it wasn't them.'

'Was it Mummy?'

' "Mummy"?'

'Did Mummy phone you?'

'No. Not her. Not your mother.'

I watched his fingers picking at a loose thread in the chair's upholstery. I knew – that ironic telepathy, the third eye seeing – something was wrong.

'What . . .' – I couldn't keep my voice steady – '. . . what is it?'

He was looking at the floor.

'Who was it?' I asked.

'What?'

'Tell me . . .'

'It's nothing,' he said.

He couldn't confide in me. Either I was too young at ten years old – or we'd all lived too long together and too far apart to risk coming as close as that.

'Forget it.'

His voice was flat, his face had hardly any colour left in it.

'You're here to enjoy yourself, Annoele. Eat up. We want to

make this Christmas special for you.'

*　　*　　*

'What are you doing, Annoele?'

Inge stood in the doorway, looking for me in the blue light.

'I'm watching 'Candid Camera'.'

Laughter filled the nursery. It was a relief to me after all the Dallas news.

'Do you want to see it?' I asked.

Inge walked inside and closed the door behind her.

'It's only funny for us,' I explained. 'The people don't know the camera's watching them.'

More laughter spurted out of the television set.

'Has my mother gone?' I asked.

'She left half an hour ago. With her friend.'

I watched the screen while Inge stood at my shoulder.

'There's a man here,' she said. 'He's come to fix the television set in your mother's sitting room.'

'What's wrong with it?'

'I'm not sure.'

Waves of laughter gushed.

'But I haven't told your mother. I want to have it fixed for her as a surprise.'

I listened with my eyes on the screen, thinking that Inge could speak as good English as any of us when she put her mind to it.

'So you won't tell her?'

'No,' I said. 'I won't tell her.'

The television audience shrieked with cruel delight at the victims' embarrassment.

'What's happening?' Inge asked.

'The man's trying to sell the ladies stockings. He keeps telling them they're so fine and holding them up. But there's nothing there. They're invisible.'

While we both looked, I thought I heard movements

83

beneath us, from the middle floor.

'I thought you said the man was repairing the television set?'

'He is.'

'I can hear him downstairs.'

'I brought the television up,' Inge replied. 'Your mother wouldn't like to think he was among her nice things, her good things. Would she?'

'No,' I said.

'Even if she found out about it, by accident.'

I listened to the pressure shifting on the floorboards; I now had ears like radar for things like that.

'Can I go and see him?' I asked.

'No,' Inge said quickly. 'No, not when he's working.' Her hand passed over my hair. 'Inside a television set is very complicated, all those wires. You might get in his way. Or give him a shock. Then the set won't get fixed and your mother won't have her nice surprise.'

'Oh,' I said.

'Or,' she continued, 'he'll fix it wrongly, and it'll go up in smoke, and hurt your mother. You don't want that?' She paused, with deliberate timing. 'Do you, now?'

I blinked at the screen.

'It's very late to come and fix it, isn't it?'

'Well . . .' – Inge withdrew her hand – 'your mother wasn't "in" today. She doesn't like tradesmen. You know that.'

'Where's she gone?'

'Someone's party. At Claridge's Hotel. Someone she knew at school.'

'Who?' I asked.

'Oh . . .' – she shrugged her shoulders – 'she doesn't tell me these things. Only where she's going – and what I'm to do with *you*.'

A new hoax was being set up on the screen.

'You have to do your homework too,' Inge reminded me. 'Not just watch television.'

'This'll be finished soon,' I said.

'Don't you mind . . .' – her voice became more confidential – 'don't you wish *your* friends could come and see you here? It would be nice for you.'

'Mummy doesn't like them coming,' I said – and I tried to explain. 'Really, it's their *mothers* coming she doesn't like. But they have to, to collect them. Only they don't come now. She thinks she has to dress up to see them. Or maybe it's for *them* to see *her*.'

'She doesn't have to do that, does she? "Dress up"?' Inge spoke above the chatter on the television. 'She's always very . . . careful with her appearance. Isn't she?'

'She thinks she *has* to be,' I said.

'Well . . . "thinking" things, that's quite another matter.' Inge's voice suggested complex adult depths.

'I don't want to see the advertisements,' I said. 'I'll put it off –'

'No,' the answer came back at me. 'No, leave it. If you like. Your mother's not here, she won't know. Will she? She won't find out. Unless I say – and I won't. It's our secret.'

'But I'll have to do my homework.' Now *I* was reminding *her*. 'Daddy tells me I have to. When he comes.'

'I'll lay it out for you,' Inge said.

'Maybe I should turn it down?'

Neither of us seemed ready to do anything about it.

'May I go down to the bathroom?' I asked. 'Please?'

'Just . . . just let the man finish what he's doing. In a minute. Can you wait?'

'Yes,' I said, quite agreeably. 'I can wait.'

The trick on the screen involved nosy shoppers opening a tin marked 'Do Not Touch!' and a spring disguised to look like a snake leaping out.

'Inge . . .'

'Yes?'

'Can . . .' – I tried speaking in a thoughtful voice – 'can I ask you something?'

'Yes.' She sounded surprised and cautious. 'You can ask me, Annoele.'

'Why do you stay with us? Why do you want to live here?' I'd always wondered. It seemed to me quite inexplicable.

'Why? To . . . to learn how to speak English, of course.'

'I don't think you need to learn,' I said. 'Not really.'

'It's good for me, living in London.'

'You don't *see* very much of it,' I told her.

'You don't have to "*see*" always. It's just something you feel.'

'I don't think *I* "feel" places like that,' I said, forgetting the question I'd asked.

'Don't you? All those countries you've been to? And going to Prague next? All those interesting places?'

I shook my head.

'Oh, I'm sure you do –'

'No,' I said, quite positively. 'No.'

I paused to think.

'Anywhere we go . . . well, it's just where we are. *Sometimes* I remember it's somewhere else and I think it's special, I try to. It depends . . .'

'What about when you're on your own?'

'I'm never on my own. Not like that.'

'With your friends, then?' Inge persevered. 'At their homes?'

'I can't stop thinking of here,' I said.

I was conscious of Inge watching me in the underwater blue.

'You're a very sad child some days, Annoele.'

I told her that was how I was made.

'It doesn't *have* to be like that,' Inge said. She sounded serious – and not troubling with her English at all, which was how she was with my mother. 'A bit of you decides for yourself. It's like history: some things – outside yourself – you can't help. Other things you *can* do – some.'

'At school . . .' I began, 'history's easy then. It's all done. I memorize the pages in my book – like a camera. All about Mary, Queen of Scots . . .'

I closed my eyes and opened them, several times, rapidly, like a camera shutter. Click – whirr – click, click.

'I can remember it that way. Which page it is and where-abouts on the page and which line.'

I did my mime again. Click – whirr – click, click.

'My father's got a photographic memory,' I said. 'That's what it's called.'

Underneath us a door opened, I was quite sure. Infinitesimal vibrations reached me, travelling up through joists and timbers.

'It's funny,' I said, 'to think we're *in* history.'

A door closed. I quite definitely heard it, through titters from the television audience.

'I think the man's finished now,' Inge said.

'Can I go to the bathroom? Please?'

I looked at Inge, whose face was set in a frown.

'You won't tell your mother, Annoele? You'll let it be a surprise?'

'She never *said* her television needed mending,' I told her.

'Well . . . maybe she didn't think you would be interested.'

I knew better, though: the nature of her mind's workings.

'Then she would just have taken this one,' I said.

I nodded to the screen, where a toy snake uncoiled and flew through the air as the tin was dropped in astonishment.

'She always said we should have two television sets.'

'You're very lucky,' Inge told me, her voice suddenly arch.

I explained to her, that's what my mother was always telling me too. As if I didn't deserve it. But she would still have had two television sets in the house. It was as if I was her excuse . . .

We both stared at the screen.

'Do your friends at school envy you?' Inge asked.

' "*Envy*" me?'

I had to shake my head.

'I don't know if they even believe me,' I said.

Worse than that, but I didn't tell her. I guessed that if they could have come here and seen how we were sometimes, or if they'd been able to see us on our 'travels' (which were supposed to be 'holidays', but were only trials for us all), they wouldn't have been able to believe any of that either. They would have realized that being the daughter of the Tomlinsons, I was deserving not their envy but their pity. For the three of us, we moved under a bad sign . . .

*　　*　　*

The next bit's a blur. I've pieced it together too many times since to know if it really happened like this or if my imagination has coloured it so . . .

We left Prague early: fact one. Fact two: somewhere after Brno my parents blew up.

My mother was complaining about Kensington.

'. . . all Annoele's schoolfriends. It's claustrophobic.'

'You're imagining it,' my father told her.

'Oh, I am, am I? You're never there, how would *you* know?'

'I'm never there?' he repeated after her. 'No, I'm not. I'm *affording* it, that's why.'

'*I* see,' my mother said, bridling.

'I'm having to work for it.'

'*I* see. And I *don't* work? Is that it? I've nothing to do with my time – except imagine things?'

'Don't you believe I do?'

'It's all you ever tell me. How hard you work. I expect it has something to do with your past, doesn't it? Surbiton, cosy Surbiton – the work principle.'

' "Ethos",' my father corrected her.

'Got to work, got to get on.'

'I got to Cambridge . . .'

'. . . and your precious double first . . .'

'You haven't done too badly out of it,' my father told her.

'Oh no . . .'

'I work to keep you comfortable. Both of you.'

'And you grudge us that, do you? *You're* working. So what are *we* doing . . .?'

Her voice trailed away, as if she realized there was no

wisdom in her asking such a question.

I thought my father looked pained in the silence that followed.

'I don't think –' he said, 'I don't think I want to know the answer to that.'

'And what does *that* mean?' my mother was obliged to ask, but less indignantly than she was used to doing. She was looking out the side window.

'I don't know how you can say that.' My father spoke slowly and the sound of his voice made me feel afraid. 'How the hell can you say it? What *you're* doing?'

Silence again. My mother's face was stone.

'I don't want to discuss this,' she told him.

'No, I'm sure you don't. *You* mentioned it,' he reminded her.

'I don't want to discuss it, thank you.'

'So fastidious, are we?'

'Not in front of our daughter.'

'Our daughter has a name.'

'I hadn't forgotten.'

'I thought you *might* have forgotten.'

Now she was glaring at him.

'Don't . . . don't tell me . . . what being a good mother is!' Her throat was dry, the words got caught up.

'Just . . . don't tell me!' she said.

Her face was blazing, bright red.

'Well, now . . .'

My father said it in the considering way my mother always hated. He started nodding his head.

'So you *do* take your duties seriously? Well, this *is* interesting . . .'

'Bloody Mister Marvellous. Running the embassy single-handed. What do *you* know?'

'Oh, you'd be surprised. You'd be surprised what *I* know.'

'You don't know anything. About anybody. Not the first thing.'

'And *you* do, I suppose?' my father spoke across her.

'Cambridge wonder-boy.' (It was like two soundtracks running together, or two television sets on different channels blaring out.) 'God's gift. The best thing Surbiton gave the world.'

My father ignored her abuse. 'But you're not quite smart *enough*, Laura.'

'Shut up!'

I knew it was really their marriage they wanted to talk about, to which they were always drawn irresistibly: the vehicle that carried us, the most unfathomable of all the mysteries, the pledge sworn on the Bible which they had such pleasure together in defiling.

'I'm not *motherly* enough, is that it?'

'You said it.'

'What am I supposed to be doing? Helping your career?'

My father forced a laugh. 'Some help!'

'What does that mean?' My mother's eyes widened. 'What does *that* mean?' she repeated. She stared at him proudly. 'Can't you hear me? I'm asking you a question.'

'I can hear you.'

'Unless I'm mistaken –' she said it with a treacherous little smile '– this *is* a career marriage?'

'If you say so.'

'If *I* say so?'

'Well . . .' – my father raced us into a higher gear – 'to know that we would have to go right back to the beginning, wouldn't we? Disentangle everything that ever happened to us. Who wanted what.'

'Yes, and I know how you would tell it.' My mother kept her eyes on his face and spoke with the same hauteur. '*I* wanted. And *you* gave. That's how you'd tell it, I know you.'

My father continued not to look at her. The corners of his mouth lifted into a smile.

'And do you think, Laura, I could ever know *you*?'

There was an agonizing pause. It must have lasted only a few seconds but, having to bear it, it seemed endless.

My mother turned her head away – and then back again to confront him.

'You couldn't know anything about anybody,' she said. 'Not the first thing.'

I looked up at the driving mirror, at my father. He was watching the road and his face was grave. His eyes also had a sly glint in them, which made me think no good was boded there . . .

'Do you hear?'

'Yes. I hear.'

'You couldn't *give* yourself to anyone.'

My father spoke quietly at first, he mumbled almost.

'Not like you? Not like you, of course?'

Then the words became less muffled.

'You could "give" yourself. Couldn't you? Or maybe you do? *Give* yourself? Do you?'

The words were quite audible now, they weren't to be confused with any others.

'Would you mind even who you gave yourself to, Laura? Would you? You've so much "giving", I don't expect you know what to do with it all.'

'Shut up!' she told him.

'It spills out of you.'

'Shut up!'

'Oozes . . .'

The speedometer needle wavered on the 60 m.p.h. mark. I was terrified sitting on the back seat watching it, my mother's face so contorted with bitterness that I saw her not beautiful for the first time, my father slamming his hand on the dashboard and the car rocking.

I thought we were going to cross the road and hit something coming the other way. My mother realized the danger too, and cried 'Watch out!'

That was like a trigger. Still holding the wheel, my father put his other hand on her neck and pressed on it till she was choking at him to stop.

'Get *off* me! For frigging Christ's sake!'

I'd never heard my mother say that before. Hearing it almost shocked me more than seeing my father's fingers tightening on her throat, which I'd watched so often dressed with jewels – fire opals and emeralds he probably didn't know about. (Or did he?)

Her face went grey, nearly blue. When my father took his hand away there were red fingermarks left like bruises. I was shaking, uncontrollably.

Then – the most unreal event of all – without a word my mother opened her bag and took out the scarf inside and tied it round her neck, so calmly I couldn't understand. Even the Givenchy label showed where it should, where other people see, at the back. I felt wetness in my underpants. Givenchy labels seemed as mad as my grandfather when you couldn't even be happy.

I hated myself. I was so weak, I'd done nothing to interrupt them. When we stopped for the bathroom I thought I was going to bring something up. My mother saw me and marched me out of the hotel at the double and back to the car. She meant us to forget. In the mirror in the dingy ladies' room I'd noticed her, though, removing the scarf and anxiously inspecting the marks.

Back in the car I didn't say anything and sat with my legs apart like a wishbone, looking at the mountains and the heavy afternoon snow clouds. Flurries kept hitting the windscreen and coming to nothing. It was so dark by three o'clock the cars we passed had their headlamps on. A lot of them were Tatras, driving fast on official business. I looked at the fields clustered half-way up the mountains where there were breaks in the forest and thought dismally how pretty they would have looked at any other time. I remember wondering if anything could ever be pretty again.

The worst part was at the frontier-post where we crossed.

I don't know where it was. (Again I'm trying to recall, or

maybe I begin to embellish memory . . .) The passage of years has blotted out the least significant details: place, time. Night time, I deduce, because we stopped in the glare of arc lights.

We were signalled to get our passports and visas ready, and joined a special queue for foreigners returning to the West. I noticed a man in uniform standing well back from the lights, taking photographs with a long lens as the cars drove through. Click – whirr – click, click.

My father turned to my mother.

'Have you got the passports?'

She didn't reply.

'Have you got the passports?' he asked her again.

' "Have you got the passports, *please*?" ' she said wearily.

'Have you got the passports, *please*?'

She pulled them out of her bag and slapped them on top of the dashboard.

'We only need the double one,' he said.

'I'm not your chattel,' my mother replied with a snort, a kind of whinny. She snapped shut the clasp of her bag and looked gloomily ahead at the files of traffic. Her fingers picked at the ends of her scarf. 'It's degrading to women.'

'It's a convenience,' my father said. 'That's all.'

'That's what I'd expect you *would* say.'

'I don't disappoint you in that respect, at least.'

'What respect?' My mother scowled.

'I say what you expect me to say.'

My mother snorted again.

'Of course,' my father went on, '*your* standards are so demanding. Do you –' he asked the question bitterly ' – do you suffer *many* disappointments?'

'All I said –' my mother laboured with the words '– all I said was, I want to travel with my own passport. That's all. It's a simple enough request, for God's sake.'

'All *I* meant was, it's easier with one.'

My mother snorted again. 'It's Victorian.'

'The Victorians were a most misunderstood couple of

93

generations in my opinion. They –'

'Your opinions,' my mother announced contemptuously, 'don't concern me in the slightest.'

My father nosed the car forward. I peered at the occupants of the other cars. Some of the drivers looked like businessmen; others had solemn 'official' faces. It didn't seem to be the season for family travel. Everyone else was at home: it was as if we were fleeing from somewhere or something.

'I didn't suppose that they did,' my father said. '*My* opinions.'

'Well, you've nothing to blame *me* for, then.'

'I'm not –'

'Oh yes, you are.'

'*I* know what I mean.'

'It's your tone of voice.'

'No, it's not.'

'Just listen to yourself!'

That stopped my father, as she must have intended it to. He drummed his fingers on the rim of the wheel and looked straight ahead, at the line of crawling cars. The same fingers that marshalled the papers on his desk in Prague, which had tried to choke his wife . . .

He lifted the handbrake and we moved forward, a few feet, into the secret photographer's range. Click – whirr – click, click.

'This is a disgrace,' my mother said.

(If only she would keep quiet, I was thinking, she might have the better of him . . .)

'You've got to be patient,' my father told her.

'That's a statement of the obvious.'

'Sometimes things are *too* obvious . . .'

My mother gave a parched smile. 'It's like everything else in this God-forsaken, crappy country.'

I saw my father's eyes find me in the driving mirror and watch for my reaction. I sat trying to betray no feelings at all.

'It's because you haven't lived here,' he said.

'That is one pleasure I'll do without, thank you very much.'

'You really –'

She turned her head to look at him, so he would hear, so there was no mistaking.

'Nothing would induce me.' She aimed the words like bullets. 'Nothing on this earth.'

She turned back and watched the traffic in front of us. She sighed at the awful slowness of our progress: my mother, whose philosophy was never to queue for anything, it wasn't what a woman in her position did.

'It's stuff and nonsense, this,' she said.

My father drew his breath in through his teeth. Unfortunately she heard him.

'What's that in aid of?'

His mouth twitched.

'Nothing,' he said tiredly. 'Nothing at all.'

It was more than my mother was ready to take. She turned round to face him. I could see she was tight-eyed.

'Look!' Her voice too was tight, and tense. 'Look, don't fob me off!'

'I wouldn't dream –'

'All this, it's just a joke to you, isn't it?'

My father looked surprised: or he pretended to be surprised. He shook his head.

'It's anything but a joke, Laura,' he said in an earnest voice that carried no conviction. 'Anything –'

'You're . . . you're actually *enjoying* it, aren't you?' She nodded, as if to say it was all becoming clear to her now. 'I think you're *enjoying* this.'

'I never enjoyed anything less, Laura. I can assure you of that.'

'Simon Tomlinson, you make me want to vomit.'

She delivered the remark with such ladylike composure, I couldn't really believe she'd said it.

My father didn't respond. His eyes were directed at the cars in front but he didn't seem to be seeing them. The car behind hooted as the file moved yards ahead of us.

'Are we staying here?' my mother asked when the driver hooted again.

My father snatched at the handbrake. The car hiccuped, then we splashed our way forward over the slush.

There were six or seven cars in front of us. Their roofs shone under the strong arc lights like film-set spotlights. Customs officers in peaked caps were dourly going about their work. Somewhere the cameraman pointed his lens. Click – whirr – click, click.

My father opened his window a few inches. Through the gap the inside of the car immediately started to chill.

My mother pulled at her coat.

'Do we *have* to freeze?'

'I thought it was airless.' My father spoke the words like a robot in a television play or a cartoon.

'*Our* comfort doesn't matter, of course? It never matters, does it?'

'I don't think you have too much to complain about.'

'Oh,' my mother said. 'Haven't we?'

'I wouldn't complain. If I were you.'

'But that's the point. You aren't,' she said. 'You're *not* me, are you?'

'No. No, I'm not.'

His voice had risen. Even to me, sitting behind them so fearfully, it suggested things: his boredom with us – relief he wasn't my mother – pity for her.

My mother noticed too.

'How demeaning *that* would be for you, of course.'

My father sighed. 'I didn't –'

'But I quite agree with you,' she said. 'Imagine! What could be worse? Being you – then having to be *me*! Sublime to the ridiculous, wouldn't it be?'

I heard all the hate in her voice and it quite unnerved me: it drove a coil of pain into my stomach and made me go hot and cold all over. My teeth were chattering, I started shaking again.

'Just –' my father began. 'Can't you be reasonable? For once? Just be that?'

' "Be reasonable"?'

'Please.'

' "Be *reasonable*"?' she repeated.

'Yes.'

'Amn't I?' She said it mockingly. '*Amn't* I that?'

'No, you're not,' my father replied angrily. 'And don't make a fool of me.'

I caught him looking at me again in the mirror, his eyes narrowed to long slits.

'I'm sure you're quite capable of doing that for yourself,' my mother told him, lightening her mandarin tone. 'Making a fool of yourself. You don't need *me* to.'

'Shut up, woman!'

He shouted it at her. I felt a knife was twisting in my stomach.

'Well, well . . .' My mother came back at him. 'I think we're losing our diplomatic head,' she taunted him. 'Aren't we now?'

'Shut *up*, I said!'

My father brought his hand banging down on top of the dashboard. I shut my eyes, I didn't want to know if people were seeing, watching our terrible son et lumière.

'No one,' my mother yelled at him, '*no one* says that to me!'

'I'm telling you to!'

'No one . . .'

'Shut up, Laura!'

'You bast –'

'Keep your mouth *shut*!'

I was sure he was going to hit her, hit her and hurt her, I was sure . . .

I suppose quite simply I must have panicked. I opened my door and jumped out before they could realize and then I just started running.

I ran back, across the tarmac, faster than I'd ever thought I

97

could. I ran past the first huts we'd come to – then I went veering off, away from the lights.

I headed for the fields, the open land, still white with the week-end's snow.

I could hear men's voices and footsteps behind me but I kept running. I think I knew I wouldn't be able to get clear of them and into that blackness – but I had to get away, I knew that too, I had to try, I just *had* to get away . . .

It was a piercing, terrified scream from my mother that stopped me, freeze-framed me.

I was in mid-stride, balanced on one leg. I spun my head round.

There, under the battery of arc lights, I saw maybe a dozen men in uniform. They were standing in two lines, they had their rifles raised to shoulder height, they were aiming at me.

Another six inches . . . if I'd gone on running another second . . . I would have been dead.

'Minefields, they're minefields!' my father whispered at me softly, leading me back and trying to calm my hysteria. I saw my mother a few yards away, sobbing into a handkerchief and being comforted by a woman with Heidi plaits.

Then I screamed, how *she* had done. Without knowing why: I screamed and I couldn't stop. Louder and louder and high enough to shatter glass. In a way I wanted to be dead and I remember being so glad too that I wasn't, I was happier than I'd ever been. I wanted to forgive them both and everyone else – the men with the rifles as well – just because I could feel something so strongly and because I wasn't dead. I choked on my screams. I told them out loud, coughing on the words, that everything would always be pretty, always.

After I don't know how long, my euphoria passed. I was carried back to the car exhausted. My father laid me gently on the back seat. My mother got in beside me, her face red with crying and the scarf dishevelled and her neck still bruised. 'My God . . .' she kept saying, 'oh my God . . .'

My father started the car and drove us with great tenderness. I felt another wild surge of happiness just knowing we were somewhere else now. I began deliciously to lose consciousness. I couldn't see anything above me through the windows except the darkness that covered the whole world – but Austria was there, I knew, because my father told me so continuously to reassure me, and I needed to believe him so much. My mother was blowing her nose. My father was telling me 'We'll buy chocolates. Boxes of chocolates. Just for you.' I pictured the mountains I'd seen on another holiday, like the Baroness von Trapp's, with their jigsaw of fields and patches of forest almost black by comparison and torn clouds ripping on their snowy height. Like those Ingrid Bergman climbed in *The Inn of the Sixth Happiness*, leading the orphan trail.

The mountains were up there behind me, and so I slept.

*   *   *

Aldeburgh with its biting easterlies and its flat leaden skies and its history of high-water tragedies was like a stage-set custom designed for their quarrels.

One day the violence in the air was more than I could take and I made my escape from the house and ran off.

Off across the roaring shingle where the sea sucked and dragged and the pebbles shrieked. A scramble up on to the esplanade, then past Benjamin Britten's house and on to the Moot Hall the Tudor men built, perched high on its stilts.

Up the outside staircase of old, salty timbers and into the museum's paraffin warmth.

Sometimes they brought me here, for culture's sake, or because the rain caught us without umbrellas. I thought I knew what was what in the glass cases: the fossils – the Iceni booty, the stone head of Claudius from Saxmundham – the Elizabethan hawking gauntlets – the Witchfinder's lantern.

In the back room that day something not in a case and which I hadn't seen before caught my eye. According to the card pinned to the wall beside it, it was the tail feather of a bird of paradise. Once it must have been glorious, shot with shades of gold, but now it was dusty and faded. The card explained (I returned on future days and memorized the gist) that in New Guinea the owning of such objects is held to be a token of a person's rank and estate. Wealth there is a concept quite foreign to the Western one: social standing in that community relates to means, but is calculated not by how much one owns but by how much of that one gives away, to the needy and deserving. The bird of paradise feathers are a substitute of sorts, an emblem: they represent that wealth but don't interfere with its capacity to work good. So the card said, and I could only presume it was the gospel truth – even though I had the feeling that not all the information was there that might be, that an essential point or two were missing for a full understanding.

Meanwhile Mrs Simmonds in the front room had rung up the cottage and I watched from the steamy window as my handsome father came sprinting along the front in his camel coat and foulard scarf to collect me. I tried to show him the feather as he took my hand but he didn't care to see. He smiled to Mrs Simmonds, thanked her, and said we had caused her enough bother for one day. 'We were terribly worried,' he told her.

Outside, on the sea-washed staircase, he let go my hand.

'You didn't see the feather,' I told him, quite sourly. 'It was lovely . . .'

'What?'

'The feather.'

He hadn't been listening.

'Inside,' I said, 'there was a feather . . .'

'A feather? Is that all?'

'But . . .'

'If it's a *feather* you want . . .'

When I reached the bottom of the stairs, he took my hand again.

100

'Why didn't you say?'

I saw *he* certainly didn't understand, not at all. And I had no clue how I could make him.

'It doesn't matter,' I said sulkily.

'How many feathers do you want?'

'I don't want any.'

'I don't think you know *what* you want!' he said. He was smiling. 'Do you?'

Oh, but I did: I did. I couldn't have explained to him, but I knew. It wasn't feathers, and he was wrong to suppose it was anything that money could buy. If feathers had been the total of it, we could have afforded to live like princes and princesses, knee-deep in them.

'Peacock feathers are nice,' he said. 'You can buy them in Liberty's.'

'But . . .'

Didn't he know? Even I knew, from watching Armand and Michaela Denis on television, from seeing Inge shiver one day as we passed some in the doorway of an Indian restaurant: come too close to one and you tempt that indigo eye of mischance . . .

* * *

When I woke up my mother was asleep, and my father had stopped the car and was outside smoking. It said some time after five on the little clock in the fascia.

I sat up. My sleep had been like oblivion. Now the fields were covered with mist. It was perfectly still. I looked at my mother beside me. She still wore the Givenchy scarf with the pattern of gondolas; the collar of her sable coat was up, protecting the scarf, and I couldn't see her neck and the fingermarks. I was so relieved her face was beautiful again I just wanted to touch her, find the skin on her throat and smooth it.

My father coughed in the dawn cold and began to walk back. He looked haggard and drawn, not how I liked him when I showed my friends at school my photographs of him. He smiled when he saw me, not very confidently. I tried to smile, but not for the first time in my life I didn't trust his eyes. They couldn't really hold me. From a distance they shifted, narrowed, looked away.

He didn't come any closer. He turned, then walked off again. I panicked. Not like before. The danger now was watching him go. I didn't want him to leave us. I also needed to know 'who are you?', all those different men he was.

He didn't abandon us, not this time. It might have been better if he had, there and then, and it would have been done with. But, if he had, I wouldn't have had the comfort of those next few hours: I count my blessings too, you see.

He drove us on to Salzburg and the two of us sat in silence in the back holding hands, mother and daughter, looking for the valleys lost beneath us under the parapet of motorway. Even in the state I was in, it was a spectacular journey in the cold pink light of a dry December morning. Frost crackled on a scattering of snow on the central reservation and gleamed like polished glass. I screwed up my eyes and pictured what the Jaguar must appear like from outside, whistling along like a torpedo.

The road was empty except for the car and us in it. My father turned on the radio, I suppose to make talking unnecessary. The needle swung behind the lit window, it was like a little red wand – sweeping over all the channels in the world, it seemed. Voices called, notes of songs and words of speech paralysed from their sense. All clamouring to say something and make an emotion felt. Petula Clark, Brel, Esso, Leningrad, 'Down at the End of Lonely Street' . . .

At last he found a station with classical music. There was some singing – duets in French – then an announcer solemnly introduced a record programme of Schumann's keyboard works. My mother said 'Excellent!' under her breath – with a brave pretence of good humour – and leaned back.

A piano started playing. I had my hand inside my mother's but I sensed that it didn't really mean what it would have meant to other people having it there. I didn't feel unhappy that she did it only as a gesture. I noticed my father watching us both in the driving mirror under cover of the music: she was holding my hand where he could see, on top of the armrest in the middle.

The music seemed to carry us. My mother felt placid, still. I looked at her when I could, moving my head round very slowly. She was how she always appeared to me when I spectated from my bedroom at home: cold, shining, unapproachable, like the face on a magazine cover or a model in a fashion advertisement – made for other people's lives, not ours.

The music rippled away like water; trilled back again, crescendoed quickly, raged, broke like a flood; subsided as it had come, from and back to almost nothing. My mother smiled to herself enigmatically and I saw my father's face cloud in the mirror. Later I noticed his fingers whitening on the steering wheel, they clutched it so tightly.

*   *   *

The night before we'd set out from London I wasn't able to sleep.

I tried to fall into the rhythm of Inge's heavy snoring from next door but it didn't work. When the clock on the corner of the square had chimed twelve times I pulled myself up on the pillows. The light on the landing was still on, shining through the keyhole. (Or maybe I was really half asleep after all, and when I got up and floated out into the hall and then down a flight of stairs I was in a kind of dream . . .?)

However it happened, I found I was standing on the floor beneath the one I slept on. I noticed that my mother's door was open; and the door beyond that, into her bathroom. I saw our cases lined up in the corridor, packed and ready for Mrs

Taylor's husband to carry downstairs in the morning.

I glided past, along the passage, and into my mother's bedroom. The woolly white carpet was like sand between my toes. I heard water tumbling into the bath and I hesitated about going on any further. Little bubbles of air whistled up my throat.

I crept across, as carefully as I could, to the bathroom door.

Till then I'd never seen my mother completely nude, and I felt a sharp stab near my heart. (What was the pain? – my father's agony at seeing her again?) I was familiar enough with the geography of most of her body by now. Most of it. In the holiday snaps I passed around at school she wore pastel-striped American bikinis under open towelling beach gowns that showed the thrust of her ample breasts and her big, tense button nipples. People on beaches would always turn round and stare, she carried about with her such a physical authority.

I stood in the dark. She lay in the bath in front of me soaping herself with easy strokes, smoothing the skin on her tanned belly. It was an eighteen-year-old's body, a woman's half her age. She had a radio on, turned down low: tuned to pop music. The vibrations of Anthony Newley's voice made the speaker rattle in its case. Anthony Newley – instead of my father's King's College Chapel records of carols and readings she played when her guests and Inge and I were there to hear.

I doubt if my father was entering her considerations at all at that moment. Her nipples had risen up like stalks. She discarded the sponge and moved downwards from her belly with her fingers making impulsive massaging movements. She rode beneath the water and I had a glimpse of her furred fork, just for a second before it was covered again. Her fingers played over it, discovered the exact spot, and sank in. The record faded and I heard her moaning with pleasure, her hips twitching under the foam.

The shrill bright light in the ceiling seared inside my head and made the room seem to spin as I drew back, into the shadows. Newley became the news instead, staccato headlines, and I saw what was happening, that the world was turning on its dark side . . .

The hips thrashed. I felt the hand-hold from before, pressing on my chest, the fingers of a steel gauntlet locking then ripping into me. The bubbles of water became a little jet rushing up in spurts into my throat.

*　　*　　*

We reached Salzburg in the afternoon, trailing the snow-clouds with us. Two o'clock was as murky as dusk and every-where was lit, and the steep, high-walled lanes up to the castle on the rock felt mysterious and thrilling.

I was endlessly cheered as we drove uphill and downhill and then through the streets of the medieval town, the tiredness lifted from me, I had the sensation I'd been sluiced out inside. (It *was* just like a fairy tale, the comparison my mother had used half a dozen times when she was describing our journey to the barber in Harrods: the places we would visit belonged to fairy tales . . .)

We crossed the fast aniseed-green river and left the car outside the hotel and from there – miraculously restored, and with all that had happened in the day cancelled from our minds – we started walking.

Is there anything I don't remember of Salzburg?

In the baroque town there were stars of coloured bulbs on wires across all the streets. In the squares the fountains had frozen over, and the prancing stone horses looked fantastical with their manes and tails of spiked ice. Buggies passed us with real horses and liveried drivers and intrepid passengers wrapped against the cold in travelling rugs and shawls. I turned round on the pavements and waved at them I was so bedazzled, and the people in the back unstuck their blue faces into slightly sheepish grins. I ran from shop window to shop window and I almost forgot I'd nearly died at the border post. I

105

danced in the yellow shine. There was a window full of mechanical toys and another one with a huge white model of the Hohensalzburg on its rock in icing sugar. Carollers holding lanterns sang above us on a balcony.

We came to the blazing lights of Tomaselli's and we went inside and had tea and brioches with Alpine honey. I remember how warm it was and the rooms being full of elderly, rich-looking women in tweed suits with velvet collars, grey-haired under their green felt Tyrolean hats. (They can't all have been like that, can they?) One lady tipped a pot of hot chocolate over herself and wept at the disgrace. I caught my mother giving her a scathing look: she who seemed to imagine that public places like cafés and restaurants were provided as theatres for our emotions, the worst ones. Maybe, though – I'm saying what I think now – she saw herself in a moment grown old, humbled to the same sort of shame and suddenly baulking at the spectacle of emotional incontinence? Age is meant to connote wisdom: to live so long and still be so frail at the end of it, so in the thrall of circumstances . . .

※　　　※　　　※

My grandfather sat in his wing chair, at my mother's request. She was breezing round the room, preferring to keep mobile. I stood stiffly between them both, straight-backed, arms at my sides, mouth sucked in, with a picture in my head of the lantern-jawed Easter Island statues I'd seen on 'Zoo Quest'.

'You came all this way?' my grandfather asked again in his wondering voice.

'I told you, Father. Do please listen,' my mother said irritably. Then she repeated the reason why we'd come, but managing to say it more pleasantly. 'We're house-hunting, sort of. Cadbury way.'

'You – came all this way?'

My mother preferred not to hear.

'Give him your present, Annoele.'

I lifted my arm and held out my gift.

'Annoele has done a painting of the house. Do you like it?'

'*This* house?'

He always spoke so slowly, as my mother would speak to him so quickly.

'*Our* house, *our* house. In London.'

'I don't know *your* h—'

'Do you like her painting?' My mother nodded at me to go forward. 'She did it herself.'

'In London?'

'No,' she called across to me, 'don't put it on his lap. Put it on the table.'

'You came all this way?'

My mother smiled grimly, as if she couldn't believe things were going so badly.

'We've just popped in. Annoele,' she called over to me sharply, 'don't touch anything!'

'Tea?' my grandfather suggested from his troubled world, rubbing at his knees.

'We can't stay long,' my mother said, at break-neck speed. 'I'm sorry, it's the drive. It's a long way.'

He repeated her, very slowly. 'A long way . . .'

'When they build a motorway,' she said, 'it'll be better.'

'You'll come – then?'

I saw my mother look at her father with a new suspicion – that he knew quite well the sense of what he was saying.

'Isn't your garden nice?' she exclaimed. 'Who does it for you? Bluebells. Look, Annoele. And lily of the valley, I can smell. An old-fashioned garden. We don't see many of *them* in London, do we?'

'In London?' He said it with more of his awe.

'We have the gardens in the square, of course,' my mother explained at the rapid-fire speed of before, although she must have known that explaining anything was useless: my grandfather had a memory like a sieve, only ancient sediment didn't slip through the mesh. 'They're private. It's not a flowery garden, though. This is. Nice and flowery. Old-fashioned.'

The smile reappeared on her face, false and ferocious.

'Don't touch, Annoele!' she almost shouted. 'I've told you, *please*!'

'Annoele?' he repeated.

'Of course "Annoele"!' Suddenly she was impatient. 'You're being so awkward, Father!'

He sat mouthing my name, seemingly impervious to the rest.

'She's done you a painting.' My mother stood trying to still herself. 'To remind you of us.' She snatched it up and waved it in front of him, but keeping her distance. 'Do you like it?' she asked him sternly.

'In London?'

'And we can think of your lovely old-fashioned garden,' she said. 'Can you smell it, Annoele, come here . . .' – her voice was warning me – 'come here and stand beside me.'

She guided me away with her hands. I could feel the strength of her resolve in them.

My grandfather beamed.

'T-t-tea?'

'We can't.'

I heard the croak of exasperation in my mother's voice.

'We can't stay. It's a long journey. It'll be much better when the motorway's built. Won't it?'

'It's a long way,' he said. (He couldn't have known about any motorway, surely?)

'I haven't counted how many miles.'

'You don't come . . .' he began.

My mother interrupted him.

'I'll count today. The miles.'

Her eyes swivelled round the room.

'We have to get back before it gets dark. It'll be summer time soon, won't it? Clear skies. Then the clocks will be going back again – before we know it. Oh, those long nights . . .'

'I could paint *here*,' I said, '*this* house.'

She spoke icily. 'When we get back to London, Annoele.'

'London?' my grandfather said.

'We've got a little place in Aldeburgh, did I tell you? I *must* have told you that. Aldeburgh, in Suffolk. East Anglia. We bought it. But we might sell it, move west. We *might*. I don't know, though. Probably . . . probably not. It's the distance. The distance, you see. Aldeburgh is closer. To London. But it's lowering. East Anglia is. I –'

'You've come all this way?'

'Yes.'

My mother bit her lip.

'Yes, we have,' she said shrewishly. 'Can't you listen?'

The venom returned to her voice.

'Can't you listen? Can't you understand that?'

There was a terrible pause.

' "Annoele" is a very pretty name.' My grandfather spoke quietly. 'Come here, child.'

'Annoele has had a cold,' my mother told him, inventing a lie. 'I don't think she should.'

'Come here, child.'

My grandfather reached into his waistcoat pocket.

'Take this –'

'Your watch?' my mother said, watching him gather up the chain. 'How ridiculous! She can't possibly!'

I felt I must hold out my hand, for his sake.

'Thank you,' I said.

'You can't, Father. She's so young. You're –'

'But it's stopped,' I said, feeling the object's dead weight in my palm.

'You can remember,' my grandfather leaned forward and whispered to me, 'remember the day you visited me.' (I stood in front of him wondering, is he really making fools of *us*?) 'You came *all* that way . . .'

'I'm sure she'll remember – without a watch,' my mother said acidly. 'A watch which doesn't work. Give it to me, Annoele. I'll leave it on the table – there.' She smacked it down. 'With Annoele's painting.'

'Annoele?' he repeated.

'I . . . I think we should go now.' My mother sounded close to defeat. 'We've tired you,' she said.

'Best school in the King's Realm!'

'There's a *Queen* now,' I told him.

'Of course there is,' my mother said. Her hand clasped my shoulder. 'And we've come a long way.'

'To see *me?*'

My grandfather asked it with a Mona Lisa smile. My mother looked confused, as confused as I was feeling myself.

'To see –?'

'Of course to see *you*,' she cut in. 'Now we have to be going. It's been a lovely surprise. Seeing you, Father.'

'Surprise . . .' he repeated her.

She'd retreated a few steps with me; that margin of safety seemed to make her repentant. As if there might not be such an opportunity again.

'Mrs Willis writes and tells us your news.'

My grandfather nodded, from that realm where he now lived.

'So I don't need to be here to know. You're very fortunate with her, aren't you? And you can go to church, across the field. Like old times.'

She spoke very matter of factly, her voice wouldn't permit itself nostalgia.

'What's the new vicar like? Does he ask you for advice? We saw the new vicarage. It was lucky for you you could stay on here, wasn't it? Everything . . .' – she was looking round the room – 'just as it was.'

We stood awkwardly for a few minutes more.

'Goodbye, Father.'

My shoulder received a prod.

'Annoele, say goodbye to your grandfather.'

'Goodbye,' I said – and waved.

'Don't get up,' my mother commanded him. 'We'll see ourselves out.'

110

Jackdaws cawed in the garden. We stumbled down the path, blinded by daylight.

'Wait a minute, Annoele. I want to get some air.'

My mother halted and gulped in some deep breaths.

'Mrs Willis should open more windows. It smells of cats in there. It's unhealthy. The sanitation people would have a fit.'

She shook her head. Fed again with this view, her eyes hardened.

'It ought to be reported.'

I shaded *my* eyes with my hand.

'Is that the way you went to church?' I asked. 'Down there?'

Somehow – like Venice – it seemed I might ask her today and not have to suffer so greatly for it.

'I don't remember. If it was that way or not.' She breathed in, then breathed out. 'I wasn't ever here much.'

'Did you go to church?'

'I had to. When I *was* here. My father was a vicar. An unusual vicar – but that's what he was.'

(He's not dead, I wanted to say, he '*is*' your father . . .)

'So I had to,' she said. 'I was "expected" to. I had no choice.'

She breathed in-out, in-out.

'It was just another custom – like coming home and going away again. Till later.'

'Were you lonely when you were a little girl?'

'Not at all,' she said quite haughtily. Her breathing exercises stopped. 'What a very odd question. What's brought this on, for heaven's sake?'

'I just wanted to know.'

I held the gate open for her and then fastened the latch behind us both.

'No, *I* wasn't lonely,' she said, as if the point was requiring emphasis.

'You didn't have a mother, though.'

'No,' she said. 'I didn't.'

'Or brothers or sisters?'

'No. Neither . . . well, neither do you.'

She moved her head slightly, just enough to be able to keep me in her sights.

'Lonely people have something wrong with them,' she said. 'In the city you can't be. Not lonely. You get to know so many people, people like yourself. There's always something to do – somewhere to go.'

She walked on ahead of me, advancing purposefully, and I had to take longer paces to keep up.

'It's not good . . . it's not good even to think about it.'

I waited a few moments before I tried again.

'Is this where you always stayed?'

'What?'

'Did you always live here?'

'Yes. For as long as I can remember.'

She was slowing, and half-turned herself round to observe me.

'What's all this in aid of, Annoele? How inquisitive you are.'

'It's nice here,' I told her, saying what I thought. 'In Dorset.'

'You wouldn't rather be here, would you? How I had to be? Spending your days in a dark, smelly thatched cottage?'

She laughed at such an absurd idea – how actresses in crinolines laughed at society balls in films, like Greer Garson in *Pride and Prejudice*.

'I preferred going places. With my schoolfriends. With their families.'

I watched her look back the way we'd come, to the house.

'Thatch is awful. It's too hot in summer, it's crawling with flies. And in winter things rustle about in it – birds and mice.'

'It's so pretty here,' I persisted. 'It's like a calendar picture.'

' "Pretty"? Didn't you hear me?' she said sharply. '*You* haven't *lived* here.' Her shoulder twitched, as if she was shaking me off. 'You don't know anything about it. Nothing.'

I followed her down the muddy lane, with its ruts and stones and ridge of wet grass between the wheel tracks.

'I wanted to live in London, Annoele, for *your* sake. To give you the best. There's always something going on there. You couldn't be lonely, it's impossible.'

She looked back at me, over that twitching shoulder. She studied me in my Harrods finery and I saw the old irritation return.

'You should try to be more grateful, Annoele. Why can't you be? Thousands of girls would give their eye teeth to have a chance like yours, let me tell you.'

I tried – I really *did* try – to look grateful, I prayed that my face would show it, to appease her, to bring us together.

'I am,' I said.

'I should *hope* so. Don't forget in future.'

'No,' I said. 'I won't.'

We walked on, in jungle file, my mother in front. I timed my strides with hers.

'Are we going to live in Cadbury?' I asked quickly as a diversion.

She shook her head at that.

'It was just an idea. I was discussing it with some people. They'd moved down.'

'The man who showed us round the cottage?'

'That was someone else.'

She walked a few steps more, skirting a puddle, then she stopped.

'I'd forgotten, though. It's so far away.'

'What?' I asked.

'Here. It's another world.'

She stood in her pencil heels and considered.

'Those are coombs.'

She pointed at the dips under the grassy hills which surrounded the village.

'If you climb one hill, you'll see another one just beyond. And another beyond that.'

I tried to imagine it.

'There's no real height, no prospect. I'd forgotten.'

She was speaking further than to me, where *I* stood. She

addressed another person, someone who'd been caught in a specific set of circumstances and had had to make her escape.

'The horizon just repeats itself. On and on and on. You get trapped. You can't see, to anywhere else. It's worth anything, just getting away. They used to say, living here – it addled people's brains . . .'

*   *   *

We were staying at the Hotel Österreichischer Hof in Salzburg.

It was new since our last visit and very modern. A disc on the wall beside the plate-glass doors said 'Grand Luxe' and, inside, the lounges with their tasteful grey and white decor had perfumed pine-cone fires and bowls filled with winter fruit on the coffee tables, waxy red apples and tangerines still in their yellow tissue paper. The clientele was very grand, and I saw my mother immediately responding.

We were lucky with views this time: we had rooms with picture windows directly above the river looking across to the old town. It started to snow lightly in the early evening and the panorama from my bedroom window when I was getting dressed for dinner was like a Christmas card come to life, with the multicoloured lightbulbs blinking and the fir trees I'd looked up at roped to the fronts of buildings now floodlit and all the tourist carriages sporting lanterns as they went bowling through the streets. I hugged myself I was so happy that at the close of this particular day there could be beauty like this still in the world.

Later my mother came in.

'What are you doing?' she asked.

I put my pen down and held up my leather-bound diary with its lock Inge had given me for my birthday.

'Oh.'

She must have noticed the way the page was crammed with print.

'That must take you hours,' she said. She forced a smile.

114

'Not really.'

'No?'

'I write it very quickly. So I remember it all.'

'You "remember it all"?'

Her lips drew together and made a queer little funnel for air.

'Over here, Missy. I'll do your hair for you.'

I turned the tiny gilt key in the lock and put it into my pocket.

'Where are your bows?' she asked. 'The pink velvet ones.'

I picked them up and handed them to her.

'Sit down, please, or I can't see what I'm doing.'

I sat on the chair in front of the mirror on my dressing table. I shut my eyes tight.

'I can smell . . .'

'Lily of the valley,' she said. 'It's by Worth.'

I opened my eyes. I tried not to look at her in the mirror, to keep it a treat in store. All I permitted myself to see was the surgery she'd done on the mark, on the arch of her neck.

'Like the flowers in grandfather's garden?' I asked.

She was silent while she brushed.

'Your grandfather's not very well,' she said at last. 'He doesn't live in that house any more.'

'Is he ill?' I asked, concerned.

'I suppose he is.'

'Is he in hospital?'

'He's being looked after. He's in a home. It's best for him.'

'Where is – '

'Anyway, I'm sure – I'm sure he's not thinking about *us* just now.'

There was a tremor in her voice that was a caution to me.

'So let's not do it with *our* evening. And waste it . . .'

She stood back to inspect her handiwork.

'Isn't this a lovely hotel?' she said, taking the brush to my ends. 'You've got a *super* room, haven't you? I never stayed in anything like this when I was your age.'

'Is it very expensive?'

'I expect so. But that's your father's business,' she told me, in a different tone of voice that meant she wasn't interested and the subject, like that of my grandfather, was closed. 'Now, turn over to this side. Head over . . .'

I obliged.

'Just –' she had only one word more left on the matter '– just so long as you're grateful.'

'I am.'

'Good. Because you're a very lucky young lady, you know.' She replaced the brush and picked up the bows.

'You mustn't –' she said it almost casually '– you mustn't do anything like that again. Running . . . running away . . .'

Out the corner of my eye I saw she was watching me in the mirror.

'Do you hear now? *Ever* . . . It's very ungrateful – to your father and me. Tonight could –'

She bunched the hair over one ear, to fit the bow on to.

'Well, we have to celebrate tonight, don't we? Head up! Arriving in Salzburg.'

She arranged the bow in place.

'Smile, Annoele! Come on, you can smile broader than that! That's better! There, it brightens up your whole face! It brightens everyone up!'

I watched her fingers fasten the other bow. They were supple and fast: thin, creamed, but also strong-looking like my father's.

'Don't you like your hair now?' she asked me. 'The bows match the pink in your dress.'

She stood back and admired the effect. I was pleased to think *she* was pleased, that the result justified her efforts.

'Are you ready?'

'I'm ready,' I said.

'Good. We'll go down now. Will you take my hand? We'll go downstairs together. When people look at us, they'll see the two of us.'

'They won't see *me*,' I said.

'Yes, they will.'

Her face became more solemn. There was such attention in her expression that I knew she understood my meaning.

'Yes, they will, Annoele. I'll be holding your hand. You're my daughter: *they*'ll see.'

She was attempting not to look about her as we came down the last flight of shallow stairs into the foyer and her heels rang on the white marble floor, but I could tell from the tension in her fingers and wrist that she was wound up for the occasion.

My father kissed me on the brow – to suit my mother's elegance – and we made our way, I between my parents, towards the dining room.

We were shown to a round table by a window and I saw my mother checking her appearance in the glass before she sat down. The marks mightn't have been on her neck at all, she had so expertly covered over the evidence with powder. I looked and took my fill, because I was feeling so proud of her.

Heroically she was wearing her Hartnell dress, plain turquoise taffeta with bare shoulders. Normally when she was going out with her gentlemen friends she wore jewellery with it, but tonight she had nothing. For some reason she reminded me of Cinderella in a pantomime before the fairy godmother waves her wand. She maybe imagined it gave her a more erotic kind of dignity, with no glitter to detract from her exposed bosom. When she tilted forward to read the menu, I saw she had nothing on beneath. Her breasts still had the low tan mark left from the summer.

My father eyed her possessively throughout the meal – how he used to and I could almost forget he had. It was embarrassing – his show of lust, her coy uncaring – and I felt, very curiously, older than both of them. Of course everyone else at the other tables was noticing us too. My mother gazed across the river to the lights as if what the rest of the room was thinking couldn't have mattered less to her.

Illuminated from the windows, people down on the public

117

river-walk outside looked up, their faces warmed by the sight. We must have seemed like one of the window displays I'd gawped at in the afternoon running from one shop to the next – like the mechanical monkeys and bears on their rotating plinths or the countless holy families, heads ringed with haloes.

Now, to my eyes, it was my mother in her shiny turquoise who had the rare, luminous glory of a saint.

Here also, in the tastefully modern green and white dining room of the Hotel Österreichischer Hof, among the stalactite lights and the sprays of hothouse orchids, something happened to savage the calm. I don't know how it started. The flare-up was so sudden I didn't even get a chance to single out a cause.

The situation exploded out of all previous proportions. It was performed for us like ballet. My mother began, serenely tossing her wine at my father, glass included. The glass crashed to the floor and the wine ran down my father's face on to his suit. He pushed the table at my mother. She sprang up just before it toppled over. Some food splattered up on to her dress and she shrieked. She kicked her chair away and grabbed the end of the cloth, so that everything went scattering across the carpet.

All the while I was pinned to the window, stunned by it. They would have started fighting, I think, if the maître and the waiters hadn't run across and moved them apart. People in the room were standing up; they'd been shocked into silence at first but now they were shouting indignantly. My mother walked off not hearing and my father more clumsily after her, treading on the broken plates. Waiters were already picking the food off the carpet. Dustpans and a carpet-sweeper appeared in seconds: a fresh linen cloth was cracked open and shaken loose. The maître with a stern expression on his face directed operations and said not a word. It was just like the scene after an accident.

Nobody remembered to save *me*, though.

I turned round. Tourists passing by outside had stopped,

seeing something was badly wrong, and made a second audience out on the terrace.

I turned my back on them. Facing the room again, I felt its hostility for the three of us. Now it was all focused on me. I saw the faces like blurs, watching me.

I tried to be composed and dignified, how my mother had wanted to look. I couldn't though. I tried, and I couldn't. Then I began to cry.

I cried quietly at first, but gradually I felt my hold of myself go. After a time my sobs were shaking me so hard that my shoulders went into a spasm and I thought I must have a devil in me. I started to scream and it seemed to be my mother's screaming at the border-post I was hearing from inside me. I was so frightened at that I couldn't do anything when hands finally led me away.

Near the door I heard American voices saying it was a scandal, parents like mine should be put in a prison.

*   *   *

I read in the *Children's Newspaper* that December 25th is the birthday of the Romans' sun god, called Mithras. It also said that Christmas used to have nothing to do with children. It explained that the stout and dependable figure of Santa Claus is derived from a Carthaginian giant who used to eat children and was presented with them as gifts from parents grateful to secure their own safety.

I heard on 'Blue Peter' that in Austria 'Krampus' – an imp or goblin – arrives every Christmas-time to tick off the bad children, the kind who are for ever up to all sorts of mischief. Shortly afterwards crimson-robed and silver-bearded Saint Nicholas makes his appearance; he carries a sack, which is brimming with eatables to reward the children who've either resisted temptation or, on Krampus's advice, renounced the folly of their ways.

119

One aspect of it all I didn't understand: each new year the children had the option of bad or good before them – they could choose to behave well, or else they could persist in their japes and tomfoolery (and possibly – the third choice – recant at the last moment). What was clear to me was that the constitutionally 'bad' ones would continue to delight in their naughtiness, not heeding Krampus and finding their reward in however much mayhem they could kick up: I understood and could make sense of that. But wasn't it also the case that the 'good' ones and the penitents were taking it on trust that they would win *their* prize too? So didn't that make the 'virtuous' children mercenary, and just as wilful in their own way, acting in a certain manner because they knew they were bound to gain as a result?

*　　*　　*

My parents had been asked to move out in the morning, so we had breakfast in our rooms and left Salzburg very early.

My mother walked smartly out of the hotel in her sable coat and a Lanvin headscarf and dark glasses. She made me think of film stars I'd seen on television newsreels and, like them, she looked too aloof to want to talk to anybody. (At such an ungodly hour there were very few people about to see us or to talk to, but that's beside the point maybe.) My father, with his professional instinct for the diplomatic gesture, at least managed to give the night porter a chilly smile.

I ran after the two of them – or tried to – carrying the unwieldy cellophaned gift of fruit and nuts I'd woken to find by my bedside. I didn't know whom to thank for it, so I hadn't thanked anyone.

The present in its cardboard scallop sat beside me on the back seat of the car. The cellophane was stretched very tightly and squeaked when I ran my fingers over it. My mother slammed her door twice and looked over her shoulder disapprovingly, so I stopped. She was still wearing her Lanvin scarf and the dark glasses.

My father waited with consummate politeness till he sensed we were both ready, and then we moved sedately off, the three of us, like royalty or like Hollywood brahmins. Only the empty streets and the pink of dawn behind the domes and spires reminded me we were in disgrace.

After Salzburg I lost track of where we went. 'West' was all I knew. (Had we had the foresight and the daring, another one hundred and eighty miles on the 'A1' in the opposite direction would have taken us to Vienna, where we could have waited till nightfall and gone charging through the museum of Freud memorabilia on a torchlit rampage, vandalizing the glass cases, sending their wares smashing . . .)

The only thing my mother said for the first half of the morning was when my father asked if she could trace our direction on the map. She told him, 'I don't read in cars. It makes me sick.'

I saw his face hardening in the mirror.

'How many bloody cars do you travel in, then?'

She didn't reply and I felt the victory was hers, however much I suspected my father's rightful interpretation of so many past events only half guessed at.

As the signs on the autobahn told us how far we'd travelled from Salzburg, I remembered random incidents in the disturbed Tomlinson family history. My father telling my mother he'd heard a man's voice on the Ansafone tape calling her 'Laura, darling'. Other occasions when I'd seen my father's sudden and pained bafflement. Opening a Harrods account and reading some of the items aloud: two foulard ties, a shaving brush with badger bristles, gold-and-silver cuff links. Finding a fat unsmoked cigar at the bottom of a picnic hamper. Coming across a book he didn't remember buying, on the shelves of the cottage in the Cotswolds that replaced the Aldeburgh one. (I very seldom went down to Astalleigh, although

121

my mother had occasional nights there when she said she needed some country air and left me in London with Inge; once a farmer unwittingly mentioned to my father a barbecue he thought had been going to send sparks into a haystack.) There had been scenes after all these intimations of something decidedly rotten in the Tomlinson menage. I would hear my mother at first fervently deny everything; then with experience she learned to dismiss any allegation simply by ignoring it, accusing my father instead of meanness, jealousy, commonness. That would always seem to incense him more.

I recognized the look in the driving mirror: the corners of his mouth were pulled down, his eyes had sunk and his eyebrows drawn together. A twitch throbbed in his temple, which was a worse sign. Merely the physical confinement of the car frightened me – literally that. We'd never had to spend so much time with so little distance between us. A space just four foot square held us.

I was becoming deeply, deeply afraid.

After that it was a long time before either of them spoke again.

My father was the first to venture.

'I think we might give Innsbruck a miss,' he said. 'What do you say?'

My mother inclined her head away. 'It's up to you.'

'It's not *really* up to me.'

He said it as pleasantly as he could.

'Did you want to go? It's *your* holiday. We won't miss it if your heart's set on it.'

'My heart isn't set on anything,' my mother replied.

'I think you'd like to go,' he encouraged her.

'Quite honestly,' my mother told him, 'I didn't give this journey a single thought.'

She pulled her headscarf closer about her face and adjusted her sunglasses.

'All my heart's set on,' she said in a voice to freeze, 'is getting from here to London as quickly as possible. *And*,' she continued, 'I never had a "holiday" anything like this.'

Three or four miles of silence followed.

'Might I suggest . . .' – my father cleared his throat – 'might I suggest you only have yourself to blame for that.'

'You can suggest away till the cows come home . . .'

'You don't think it has anything to do with *you*?'

'I'm not thinking anything about it. I'm trying to put it out of my mind. I only want to forget these days when I get back. With luck I'll never have to think of them again.'

There was another long tense pause, lasting three or four miles.

'Tell me, Laura. Why *are* you here?'

My mother's reply was slow to come.

'It's Christmas time,' she said at last.

'Your father must –'

'He doesn't have anything to do with it!' she said impatiently. 'What does a vicar know? Anyway, I come from Dorset – I come from a pagan land.'

'Why do you believe in Christmas, then?'

'I don't "*believe*" in it.'

'No?'

'No,' she repeated. 'You're brainwashed, that's all.'

'What do you mean? "Brainwashed"?'

'It's a business. An industry. Carols for weeks and weeks. The television, the wireless. Newspapers. They all tell you the same thing.'

'What's that?'

'Well, you must have it too,' she said, fixing on the motorway in front of us. As she spoke, the tower and flank of a church appeared in the blue distance. 'The usual things. To . . . to put your house in order. Everyone . . . everyone makes up at Christmas time.'

'So we're "making up"? Is that what we're doing? Last night in the hotel . . .'

My mother sat mute and pulled out the Lanvin logo on her scarf from underneath her coat collar.

123

'Last Christmas,' my father said, 'someone from the French embassy threw himself under a train. No one discovered till January, when they found his head.'

My mother turned away and looked out the side window.

'That's horrible,' she said.

'Do you remember Davies? In Oslo? All those letters from his children he used to get in the Bag? I heard – five years ago he did it, in Petersfield of all places – he blew his head off with a shotgun. An hour before Boxing Day lunch.'

'You're inventing it –'

'I'm not! Not at all! He did it, sprayed his brains up on the ceiling –'

My mother puckered up her mouth with distaste.

'It's for children,' she announced. 'Christmas.'

'*He* didn't do much for them, did he?'

'You *would* say that, wouldn't you? You're so clever, of course –'

My father pushed his arms straight out against the steering wheel and seemed to be restraining himself from saying anything more.

We travelled on with the silence. From where I sat in the middle of the back seat the leaping silver Jaguar on the bonnet appeared to be devouring the outside lane of the motorway.

In the event we didn't take any of the signposted feed roads into Innsbruck. I knew my father wasn't really attending at all. I saw the 'look' again – the sides of his mouth dragging, his eyes sunken and eyebrows pulled together. The little vein like a crinkly wire was throbbing ominously in his temple.

*　　*　　*

'Maigret' music in the corner of the nursery. A struck match, a face illuminated like a carving. Shadows scramble up walls. Frosty railings, alleyways of dirty trampled snow. A wintry labyrinth of cold and shadows. That music. As the accordion plays, a boy in the compartment of a train slowly traces a swastika with his finger on the sweating window.

My mother has a foreign friend called Klaus: he's the most handsome man I've ever seen, even more so than the man my father once found himself sitting next to when he took me to a children's concert at the Festival Hall, who tried speaking to him. He is more bespokely dressed than my father even, whom he reminds me of with his Viking-blue eyes that are so sharp and alert, and with the same pretence of laughter and fun in his face that only surgery, surely, could have formed so perfectly.

He's allowed to come about the house, Klaus, which is a very rare privilege. His eyes record every single object in the drawing room one Sunday lunch time when we are all on our best behaviour. My mother introduces me to him, although we've been careful observers of each other on his previous visits.

'This is Annoele, Klaus.'

Instead of being obliged to look bashful, he bows. I'm rather taken aback by his courtly formality.

'Annoele,' my mother says, 'would you be a darling and pour us two glasses out of the green bottle?'

She flutters her fingers. It's a bad indicator because it suggests one of her fey moods. The depression that must follow is invariably acute.

'With ice for me, please. And cut us a little bit of lemon too, a teeny wee bit – and just a splash each from the tonic bottle? Lovely!'

I try remembering it all.

'A drink makes a Sunday civilized, Klaus, don't you think? I'm so glad you were . . . passing by. You must stay and have some lunch with us – will you?'

I have my back to them so I can't see the looks they must be trading with each other.

'I can't get the top off the tonic bottle,' I tell them.

'Here, let me,' says Klaus, who hurries across.

He loosens it with just a wrist-flick.

'Now,' my mother calls to him, 'your story again, so Annoele can hear. She'll *roar*!'

My mother isn't speaking her own vocabulary, it doesn't

125

belong to her. I know she is well adrift . . .'

'Today I was walking through the park. Saint James's Park.' She interrupts him.

'You've *walked* out here? You poor boy, you must be exhausted! Come and sit down beside me!'

Draped on the gilded sofa her eye spotted at a Phillips auction, she is being at her most actressy.

While I stand pouring, Klaus launches into the story he's already told my mother.

'I was carrying my raincoat. What happens? A duck catches hold of the end of it – and won't let go!'

'Oh *no*!' my mother squeals.

'Quack-quack-quack! There we were, it was like –'

' "Tug of war", we say. But how *awful*!'

'Quack-quack-quack!'

I can hear my mother is continuing to be hysterical.

'You poor thing!'

When I turn round and begin my journey across the parquet, she's still laughing and mopping at tears. She sees me and starts to recover, she pulls herself up on the sofa.

'Klaus first, dear. He's our guest.'

He takes his glass and bows again.

'What a hoot! Thank you, Annoele,' she says to me. 'Oh. Oh, you've forgotten the lemon.'

It's meant to sound to Klaus hardly enough to bother about, but I hear the reproach in it to me.

'Never mind, then. We'll do without.'

By the telepathic code we share, she's blaming me for trying to puncture the mood. It's as if she anticipates that this Sunday lunch time 'high' will have – mid-week perhaps – its terrible fall.

Upstairs that night Inge tells me that Klaus is no more Swiss, as he claims, than she is.

'Oh?' is all I can think of to say.

I watch 'Maigret', but the story is very complicated. Inge

scribbles a letter, to 'back home' as she always calls Denmark.

On the screen a husband has built a house like a little palace for his fancy wife. She has a tradition of inbred gentility and he has not: he craves what will make his existence special and lift it out of infecting reach of the ordinary in the town where they live. Before they married he was a local lawyer who made his peace with the Nazis, and they rewarded him well. The sound-track is a kettle-drum roll. Outside in the snowy square men from the town beat their fists rhythmically on the windows of his empty car.

'What is he, then?' I ask.

Inge sucks on her pen.

'Polish? Or from where your father is?'

'Czechoslovakia,' I enunciated very clearly.

A new complexity develops in the television story. Inge's pen scratches away on the paper. What does she think of us all, what does she write? – why does she sometimes practise her photography as my mother leaves the house, with her expensive camera, swearing me to secrecy? Click – whirr – click, click. Is she making up an album? She always locks the door of her room, I can never discover anything more about her than the little she tells me.

Klaus vanished after a shorter run than usual. A black depression waited, and my mother headed straight into it.

Inge – as instructed – took me for long walks in Kensington Gardens. We hired yachts and sailed them on the pond. We would find an empty bench within sight of Peter Pan and feed the pigeons with crusts from brown paper bags.

Once on Bayswater Road Inge cried out.

'There!' She grabbed my arm. 'Did you see, Annoele?'

'What?'

'It was *him*!'

'Who?'

'Klaus!'

'*Klaus*?'

'A big black car,' she said. 'With fins.'

'Where?' I looked round, I tried to catch sight of it.

'I'm sure it was him.'

'Oh.' I choked down my disappointment. 'I didn't . . . I didn't see him.'

'I'm sure it was,' she said. 'It's like the cars in photographs of Prague.' (It struck me that, unusually, her English seemed quite exact.) 'Very important people have cars there.'

'Was Klaus important?'

' "Important"?' She wasn't hearing me.

'You said so.' I was still looking over my shoulder. 'In a car like that?'

'It's gone now.'

'What was it?' I asked.

'I don't know.'

My eyes switched back to Inge. I watched a shrewd look on her face I didn't recognize.

'It might have been a Z-'

She stopped herself.

'A what?' I asked. 'A "Z-"?'

'A Zil,' she said. 'They're Russian.'

' "Russian"?'

'I don't know.' She was suddenly evasive. 'Maybe it wasn't him.'

We turned back. She took my hand.

'Don't tell your mother, please. She doesn't want to hear about him again.'

'No, I won't.'

I accepted her sudden command of the language, as I accepted the strangest occurrences in my life. It was something else that disturbed me, on her account: the thought that she might care for this man as my mother had done.

'Will we go and have some tea now?' she asked me.

'Are you tired?'

'It's cold. London *is* cold. A cold city.'

'I don't know,' I said. 'I've always lived here. Prague is

colder, my father tells us it is in his letters. He goes up to the mountains sometimes. They're called the Tatras, like the cars are,' I explained. 'You can see Russia from there.'

'Did he say so?'

I nodded.

She weaved us between the pedestrians.

'What is a Zil like?' I asked her. 'Like a Tatra?'

'You must forget I said it, Annoele. Pretend I didn't.'

She pressed my fingers and curled them into her palm.

'Will you?'

'Yes.'

'It will be our secret,' she said. 'Another secret. And I shall buy you a chocolate cake. And we shall go to – no, not Derry and Toms. Today – the Hyde Park Hotel! We shall live like princesses!'

She was looking at me for approval. My hand hurt.

'And not tell your mother. Like princesses! Our secret, Annoele.'

I tried squeezing on her hand holding mine, to let her know I understood this dependence on something so illusory as a man's affection.

My mother got over it, as ever.

A new gentleman friend came to collect her one evening. I watched her leave from my window, then Inge and I ate our supper in the kitchen, like two poor below-stairs maids.

Afterwards Inge made the excuse of having to look for something. Back upstairs I heard her turn the handle of my mother's bedroom door, which she often did when my mother was out – but it was locked.

I switched on the television set in the nursery. A quiz game was finishing, with big money prizes which the audience gasped at. I watched the advertisements – 'Flash' for a clean kitchen to impress your neighbours, 'Lux' soap flakes to keep your woollens looking soft – and then I turned over to 'The Dick Van Dyke Show'. 'Panorama' came on, about an island called Cuba and missiles and eyes in the sky.

Inge saw me to bed. I lay imagining rotating mechanical eyes over London, which became human eyes with a doggy, world-wearied expression like Morey Amsterdam's on 'The Dick Van Dyke Show'.

I surfaced from a dream hearing rumbling noises and I knew Inge was engaged in another of her rummaging sessions downstairs. I realized then, as much asleep as awake, we have a spy in the house.

But it didn't seem to matter greatly. It was only how we lived in these modern times.

*   *   *

We had lunch at a round futuristic building beside the auto-bahn called the Sputnik-Sporthotel. It was full of loud, over-fed Germans and Swiss on skiing holidays. We sat in the space-age restaurant, among the chrome and smoked glass and purple tweed on the walls, and we ordered Spanish omelettes. When they eventually arrived they tasted of nothing, and I choked on a piece. My father thumped my back and my mother looked away without interest, disclaiming any obligations to me. She had nothing else to hold her eyes in this place, though, and she soon lost her patience and pushed back her orange polystyrene chair on its pedestal base so hard that it toppled over.

The afternoon was painful after that, with none of us speaking in the car. We had to listen to music, endless song-cycles exchanged between love-lorn baritones and temperate sopranos, and I'd had so much I wanted to reach into the front and switch it off. The splendour of the journey – originally it was going to be everything – it meant nothing at all now. Through the glass the picture-book villages didn't look as if they could be real. I began to wonder seriously if I was dreaming them. If it was a dream, then none of the rest could be happening either.

We turned off the motorway and stopped for tea at a small spa-type hotel in a garden beside a lake. Pink stucco was peeling off the outside walls. Inside, the rooms were faded and sounded hollow when we walked across the sanded floorboards trying to find someone to give our orders to. A woman appeared from a back corridor: one of her arms was in a sling and she had a cross of sticking-plaster on her forehead. She looked as if she'd been badly knocked about. A man in a blue apron who might have been her husband served us and didn't open his mouth except to tell us the price. His hairy hands and strong stubby fingers had no delicacy for the eggshell *famille verte* china.

I saw how pinched and uncomfortable my mother was as she creaked back in her basket chair and took rapid sips of her tea. She kept watching the murky, choppy lake through the broken trellis-work. My father too seemed sobered, running his fingers up and down the creases in his trousers. I found the tea undrinkable, I was so tired with it all.

In the *Damentoilette* when I was shut inside the cubicle I started to cry again, for the sake of nothing in particular. I stayed there, locked in, till I stopped.

In the draughty hall I saw my red eyes in a misty, scratched mirror. My father and mother were waiting for me on opposite sides of the front door. Neither of them commented on my condition. When we were walking back to the car my father seemed to be going to take my hand but he must have thought better of it, and awkwardly slipped his hands under the flaps of his pockets.

The engine growled as we raced out of the car park, and I heard the gravel churning beneath the chassis. My mother was thrown against the door and looked stern and unhappy. I felt the sickness from before coming up again, and prayed it to go back down.

It started to get dark early.

At one point I turned round to look out the back window, imagining I could hear through the striving voices on the radio a sound like the rush of leathery wings being shaken out.

131

The light was fading and left the car's shadow like a stain on the shiny wet autobahn which the next shower of rain would wash away. I saw the silhouettes of our three heads inside. But there was no black bat, only a beating of wings I could make out as the tyres hissed on the road and cross-currents of wind above a ravine thumped the sides of the car and came whistling in through the quarter-light sealings.

Later – when the noise wouldn't stop and the cabin filled with yellow light – I turned and looked over my shoulder again. A car's headlamps and foglamps were being beamed straight at us. I made my eyes into slits, how my father did. I was able to identify it was a Mercedes, from the grill. It was keeping an even distance from us. The invisible driver flashed the battery of lights at us. I was thinking, it's because we're in the outside lane and he wants to pass. But my father wasn't letting him.

Its gleaming radiator was like the snarling open snout of a shark. I couldn't see anyone inside. I tilted my head different ways but it didn't help, I still couldn't see anyone. Only the dazzle of lights through rain-runs on our back window and the hard cold glare of metal in pursuit, as if the machine smelt blood.

Passing under pylons the radio caught the interference, instead of lieder we were picking up Voice of America, the latest from Washington, something about the KGB, a crackle ... There was a noise from the speaker that sounded like breath being pumped out of an enormous animal: I imagined a great green web-toed slimy Caliban-thing with stumps for arms and a head full of hate.

Eventually we lost the Mercedes.

To do it, the Jaguar had to reach one hundred and ten. A convoy of freight lorries came between us, seven or eight of them; they were lit up like ships, like liners riding the spray.

We left the motorway suddenly, with the engine whining.

On the radio a woodcutter's daughter was singing winsomely to a gamekeeper, but my ears hurt with her music. The filter road screamed under us. I shut my eyes.

If I'd only known, what it was was the world calling to us its *Abschied*, its farewell . . .

For the rest of our journey we had to suffer the menace of winding country roads taken at speed: roads with blind turns and no markings which, at the best of times, require all the concentration a driver can give them.

Patently my father wasn't up to it. The anguished, thrumming music was a sufficient danger in itself, like a knife in the head. A Jaguar car was too impatient for all the bends and loops and the single tracks and the fragile wooden bridges where the mountains come down as sheer rock to road level. The engine revved and groaned whenever it had to slow.

My mother sat with her hand holding the grab-handle. That probably irritated my father more, because he started to take the corners faster. We were climbing, which was alarming enough on those hairpin roads with barely adequate crash barriers on the off-side. It was getting darker too by the minute, and I sat in the back watching the dials and counters warming to life in the walnut fascia so that I wouldn't have to think about outside.

In the genteel glow, reminding me at first of night drives home from the country to London, I realized we depended utterly on those taut fingers pulling on the wheel; we presumed for our safety that every switchback of the road up and down was foreseen and that the proper pull or pressure was applied on each of the corners. The most minor miscalculation, a moment's distraction entering the side of my father's eye, and we would have black empty space under us. I couldn't help looking down then, into the V of valley with its cowmen's huts somewhere beneath us and a tip of lake, like a cold tongue licking the land in that thinning light.

We began to get more interference with the radio and for a

bit all we could hear was pop music. I wished we'd had that before instead of the caterwauling. My mother looked as if she was ready to perk up too: she who conscientiously spent her evenings – or parts of evenings – at operas and recitals and nothing of a lesser nature, and filled the house when her visitors came with classical piano music from my father's record collections on the radiogram.

We listened for a while. 'Love Me Do' came on. I knew my father didn't like the Beatles and he flicked the switch to 'Off' between turns of the wheel.

The emptiness felt almost brutal after that, like a loud pain in my ears. Of course, in a sense we were now beyond the aid of secondary effects like music.

We'd got away from the tourist hotels, into primitive Bavaria. After the ramshackle customs-post like a garden shed and no striped pole, we'd just kept on climbing.

I thought my father must have a destination in mind really, but if he had then we'd missed it. At a succession of crossroads he looked confused, he peered at the names on the signposts – and then drove us towards the most hopeful-sounding. But by mischance or by some malicious contriving of the sign-writer, we never reached any places.

Past our first cloud – we drove up through it like bonfire smoke – it seemed more and more unlikely that we would. There were long gravel run-outs for cars coming down, but nothing else. I thought once I saw an ibex or a chamois high above us on a shelf of rock but it might have been a goat gone wild which was just showing off, or a trick of the vanishing light. I remembered the 'Armand and Michaela Denis' programmes on television. We three were another kind of 'wild-life' altogether.

We started to come down at last – through another cloud like grey steam – and I felt my ears pop. The grab-handles were essential for the final few miles. The car rolled and pitched on the corners till I felt my strudel-slice from tea coming up. I managed to edge my window down a little way. We reached the flat just in time.

After that we ran for ages alongside a forest, on a stretch of mainish road which followed the contours of its pine wall and made me feel better. Tourist guides I've read since call those woodland wildernesses 'primeval'. Warning signs illuminated by our headlights had a silhouette of a boar with pointed tusks on them. I looked for them the little distance I could see into the sinister green, among the high narrow trunks.

The last of the light was draining by now, turning the sky sooty. It was getting harder to see anything ahead of us, even over the next hummock in the road. My father pressed some switches and more lights came on in the console. From where I was lying the night seemed to be gathering everything into itself. Maybe we would be included too, sucked in? – we belonged to the darkness?

We sped between some empty fields and I sat up to watch. We came to another forest. Inside was like a vast necropolis. I was frightened to think what might live there where I couldn't see and where the greenness blurs even in daytime to black. Perhaps further in, I thought, the boars there haven't ever seen a human soul?

'Why are you slowing down?' my mother was asking.

My father grappled with the gear lever and looked over his shoulder. 'We'll have to find somewhere for the night.'

'I saw a sign for an old inn,' I piped up. 'Back at –'

' "An old inn"! Well, this should be an experience!' my mother said witheringly.

My father turned round and looked at her, and then he glowered again.

'Have you any other suggestions? We *could* spend the night in the car.'

'No, thank you very much,' she tossed back at him. 'If we were still on the motorway we wouldn't be looking for a crummy inn.'

'You'll just have to put up with a "crummy" inn, won't you?'

'*You* seem to have decided that,' she snapped back at him. 'For God's sake, why can't you go back?'

'I thought we could cut across. We must be able to join another road to Munich.' He pointed towards Munich, or to where he thought it was.

'How do you know?' my mother asked him disbelievingly. 'How can you possibly tell that? With *your* powers of direction we're probably heading straight back to Prague.'

'We'll find a road to Munich,' I said.

'*You* say!'

My mother pretended to laugh.

'Oh, well. It's got nothing to do with me, Simon Tomlinson, I can tell you –'

'Of course not, reading maps in cars makes you sick. *You* said. I forgot.' My father's voice was a cruel imitation of how she spoke, puffing his cheeks out as if they had plums inside.

'Shut up, will you?'

'It didn't *use* to make you sick, did it?' my father said in his own voice, which was as featureless as the announcers' on the Home Service. 'Why sudd–'

'I've got sick of a lot of things.'

My father moaned.

'Oh Jesus, Jesus God, I'm exhausted. I can't take this. Not any more . . .'

'What about us? You're driving like a lunatic. Don't you care about *us*? If you –'

'Everything comes back to *me*, doesn't it? You *take* it all – but you're the first to blame, every time. You don't want any responsibilities. Do you? No, not *you*, not on your life –'

'I have responsibilities to myself –'

'To *yourself*?'

The car almost went into a skid.

'Watch the road, will you?' my mother cried at him. 'What about our *safety*, for God's sake?'

136

'I . . . Jesus wept,' he said angrily – and he asked what he always asked: 'What the bloody hell have *you* got to complain about?'

My mother covered her eyes with her hand. I sat with my fists clenched on my knees, waiting for her to say what she would. But she didn't say anything. Strangely – in that silence, with only the engine humming – I felt the victory wasn't my father's. My mother's stillness took it away from him. They shared it: or else they shared the ignominy of neither winning, the squalor of nothing gained or lost.

We stopped on the edge of the forest, at an inn made out of an old farmhouse or a mill and set beside a fast stream.

Under an early moon the water against the fields was like a gash of silver. There was a dried-up wooden wheel at the side and I thought of the miller's daughter singing.

As we approached, the inn seemed to belong to that fairy-tale province my mother had told the barber in Harrods about. Close to, it wasn't so impressive. The high steep roof sagged in the middle and there were tiles missing: the beams authentically criss-crossing on the front were flaked to the white beneath and looked rotted through. With my third eye I should have foreseen it as portentous – to suit the temper of the story I'd write one day – but I didn't.

To me the inn seemed rather beneath us, and to my mother too. She didn't even get out of the car and my father went off to inquire on his own. We both sat without speaking or moving, looking through the lit windows into the cheerless dining room. Elderly heads in a corner were bent over to eat and a waitress stood against a wall reading a newspaper. She had to lean forward to catch any light from the 1930s-ish pink glass shade like a clam shell on the panelling behind her. The current, like the company, seemed to be running on very low wattage. The heads were raised to chew and lowered to gobble again; the waitress listlessly leafed through the pages of print. Ropes pulled and plates went up very slowly on a lift in the corner. It was hypnotically tedious and I thought we'd die if we had to stay here.

My mother sighed as if somehow it was my fault, which made me feel even worse. I concentrated bleakly on the curtains: gingham with big brown and white checks like the tablecloths, and pinned back with black ties.

I held out till my father came back and solemnly informed us that they had rooms for us and we would be staying the night. Immediately my mother reached down for her handbag and sprang out of the car as if she couldn't wait for the humiliation to begin. I got out after her, looking very dejected about it, and slammed both our doors – as if I was required to make up for what she was really feeling.

My father swung round when the doors banged. His eyes watched me fiercely out of their hollows; for the nth time I saw the tell-tale vein like a flex throbbing on his temple. I smiled vaguely – how they both smiled to their friends when there was another blow-up in the offing – then I followed the trail of my mother's scent.

Inside I kept close to her because of the smell of paraffin and burnt cheese. Her expression announced it was a preposterous mistake: a bad dream, and she'd wake up and none of it would have happened.

She walked past the counter straightening her pleats. My father studiously signed the register. I felt like my mother's page.

My father followed us both upstairs – to our three rooms, not two.

The inn was archaic: the rooms had bare wooden floors and massive painted pine furniture and they smelt of sawdust as well as the paraffin and burnt cheese wafted up through the gaps where the planks didn't meet. I was fascinated by the headboards on our beds, they were like great scrolled tombstones. Lying in the middle of my mattress, worn out, hearing the two of them clattering behind the walls on both sides, I felt like an infanta.

I woke with a start when I heard their voices on only one side of me. The inevitable abuse began, words being shouted, followed by silences: then, on this occasion, heavier sounds too, like an object being dropped repeatedly and the floor shaking, and – once – a stifled scream.

Trying to ignore the jolts and shudders through the floor, I had the thought that I was really older than either of them: in my own way, even as I was, I reached beyond where *they* would ever reach.

Downstairs, at dinner with my father, I managed to smile. More wanly and sadly than before, I knew, although I had no better reflecting surface than the dim lights shining in the window to see in.

My mother hadn't come down, but I smiled enough to pardon her and to let my father realize that I absolved him too. He was looking very out of sorts and only picked at his food when our plates were brought to the table. I ate mine demurely while all the time I was wondering inside, with my thoughts like a flutter of tiny birds, how could I be outwardly so composed and have any appetite left?

I sat quite calmly studying my father to begin with, considering merely the externals, what had attracted my mother to him in the first place – Simpson's blazer, Harvie and Hudson shirt, Corpus tie, polished McAfee shoes even in a creaking, down-at-heels Bavarian country inn well out of the season – just as if I was a naturalist cataloguing my specimen. I'd always appreciated that he made an admirable companion for my mother, at least so far as appearances went: they looked well together. Now I see – even sitting there in that dining room I was aware of it to some degree – that there was so much about the man's life which neither of us could have known anything about: the War, his days before university – living in Surbiton, going to the grammar school, his parents whom I'd never seen, a sister he said he had – all his Cambridge life, the rugger tours with his college, then his friends in London, years abroad in

Lisbon and Nicosia before he married, his posting to Vienna, his nights in Prague, and (strangest and most elusive of all) that other time in our prehistory we never talked about, the year before I was born – when he was one of the delegated watchers in the Monte Bello Islands as the British A-bomb went up, an awesome new wonder for our age . . .

I don't suppose my mother could have begun to guess what he in his turn was capable of knowing about *her*. Probably in all her mischief-making she forgot something quite so obvious as this, that his was a life of information-gathering and – amassing as well as diplomacy. It was the view of his White-hall superiors (so we learned later) that he had the finest kind of brain for his business. When my mother had to entertain those grandees to dinner at Monmouth Square in my father's 'leave' time she must have thought – comparing them in her head with his younger, livelier colleagues whom she invited to her parties in his absence – that the tedium of their company and conversation must characterize *him* too and (quite illogic-ally minimize the risks of discovery.

'Discovery': at home I would notice how my mother still jumped whenever the telephone rang with an expected mess-age, when a car door banged outside, when Inge cheerfully stumbled over her syntax: 'You will be having a nice time when you leave from the house?', 'You have been with good friends, yes, until this morning?' I had to ask my friends to ask their mothers to wait outside in their cars when they came to collect me: it was partly my mother's doing – she said she needed to go and get changed to speak to them – and partly my own, because of embarrassment and to save those ever-vital appear-ances: when they inadvertently rang the bell they could see my mother through the stained glass running upstairs, shouting down at me that she'd scream if she had to talk to any of them, they were so boring.

'Discovery': it was one of the words I'd just heard upstairs through the thin wall between the bedrooms. My mother had said it, not my father. Accusing him of fabricating something.

'So clever!' 'Know-it-all!' 'Too bloody right!' he'd told her, and then I'd stopped listening. I didn't want to hear them just giving themselves away like that, all the things they'd tried to make me and everyone else think they were: my mother so proud of herself, unconcerned to be defined by other people's prejudices, beautiful in her pleated tweeds and silks, in her coldness and hauteur; my father aloof in a different way, so dependably high-minded and high-principled, above the tug of domestic things.

What earthly chance did I stand born to these two? For a few seconds I felt panicky before I remembered to smile and the sickness travelled back down again, into my stomach.

My father, making fork trails on the checks on the table-cloth, seemed baffled by my behaviour. I hadn't stopped watching him, not wanting to let him go now I had him. Sitting opposite me, with those fine strong hands I've remembered all my life, he wasn't the man I'd heard through the wall: until a sudden little rush of joy passed again – it lasted only a very few seconds – I felt I could have made him and my mother and me all different people and we might have been happy as I must have suspected we'd never really been before, or so fleetingly that the memories were like the acetylene sparks blown on to the frozen railway track. Laughing, all three of us, running down a staircase in someone's house; my mother unwrapping the ermine stole my father had had delivered from Fortnum's on her birthday and the room waist-high in tissue paper and white like snow; the three of us dancing in the hall at Monmouth Square, celebrating the news of my father's promotion to Prague.

His mouth worked, stabbing his fork into his slab of stodgy-looking chocolate cake. I tried – I *tried* – to feel sorry for him, but I must have known it wasn't the proper emotion, because I couldn't. Not then and, God knows, not now. He didn't invite sympathy. He was too self-sufficient, too respected by every-one we knew, too much of a vocational diplomat still in his London finery, sitting at the modest brown and white check-

141

cloth'd table as his Bavarian nightmare began. I couldn't plumb deeper, I couldn't empty myself for him. I was giving him back what I could – kind smiles, kind words, fingers touching when we passed butter or knives – and I knew that gestures were the sum of it. My being a child wasn't the point. He was a stranger to me, by dint of circumstances and by the nature of his sex. I think I realized then that I was more my mother's child than I could ever be his. If my mother didn't deserve me, or him, just too bad. There's a mystery in some things lying beyond words, out of reason's jurisdiction.

For a few moments my father smiled at me: it was as if he hadn't seen me all evening and he was surprising both of us the way we used to be, long long ago. It felt so odd too, sitting with him, my head was as light as a balloon floating on a piece of string: only the two of us there together, and my mother nowhere – as if she didn't exist for us now, or as if we'd never even known her.

He took me up to bed and I called him back and kissed him when he politely turned away to leave me to undress.

He smiled again, but not how he'd done downstairs in the dining room: he didn't seem to know who it was he was smiling to now, his mouth was working quite apart from his blue Viking's eyes, which were as cold to look into as those colliding ice floes we'd stood watching from the bridge over the Vltava.

Afterwards I slept very badly in the hollow of that giant mattress, which must have done service to generations. I woke before the light went out in the corridor, dreaming that the guards aiming to shoot me had really fired and that their bullets had pierced my heart. It took minutes for the feeling of being dead to clear – it was like being weighted down with sand and being punctured and the sand filtering out very slowly, like something long, complicated, intestinal.

I lay awake for a long time after that, curled up into a ball and shivering. I slept again eventually. When I woke up it was in darkness, in the still of night, thinking I'd missed my footing getting on the train and I'd fallen from it I didn't know where and I was lying uncared for and forgotten in drifts of snow with more of the same deadness in my legs.

I reached for the blankets and found them bundled around my knees. I heaved myself up thankfully: after my two burnt-cheese dreams I could feel that this was nothing less than raw life which was pulsing its way back through me.

I was even more grateful for the morning, when it came. I was woken the first time by the lowing of cattle from stalls beneath the inn. The second time daylight teased me awake: it shone through the gingham curtains and patterned flickering chessboards on the walls and ceiling.

The room as I made everything out seemed better-humoured than it had done last night. In a bizarre half-dream I looked down for my feet and imagined the high carved endboard of the bed was the front of a sleigh, speeding me across a lake of ice with bells jingling. Then I remembered I had to lie waiting for other sounds and the room seemed to shrink again at the thought – and me too with it, sunk in the dip of the bed, which was only a bed after all and not a vehicle with greased runners for the fast winter transport of infantas.

I hauled myself uphill to the edge of the mattress and yanked back the sheet. It was very cold and my breath came out as little scuds of hot steam, like my father's on the road above the river explaining to me the international decencies of river navigation. My toes felt for my slippers and I slid off the bed, pulling my nightdress down over my bottom.

They were up next door, in the room they'd been in when I lay listening to the insults and the thuds. I heard a slur of words exchanged, but nothing more. I got dressed very quickly and tugged at my hair with a brush and then I sat down on the one hard wooden chair to wait.

It was a long wait.

My father finally opened the door and he couldn't even

smile. He was dressed in more elegant, discreet un-holiday wear: a fawn cashmere jacket, flannels, burgundy mocassin shoes, a navy and white polka-dot silk cravat. It was how my mother loved men to dress: so why, I wondered, piqued at her uncaringness, why couldn't she love my father too? For once I was almost angry with her.

Breakfast was set for two again and eaten in silence. The dining room was empty and still smelt sickeningly of paraffin fumes and scorched cheese. I had difficulty managing to eat anything at all. My father seemed even more on edge than he'd been last night. The waitress watched us with her arms crossed, looking not very charitable about either of us.

I did what my mother would have done, pretended not to see her and turned my neck and head in the opposite direction. Maybe my father misinterpreted my piece of pantomime, for he got up suddenly, scraping his chair back on the floorboards, and told me to hurry up.

I gulped down the hot tea in my mouth and unstuck my legs from the rush seat on my chair. I knew from the tone of his voice that he meant business this time.

My mother was waiting outside in the cold sunshine, walking up and down. She was smoking, which she very rarely did in the morning. I must have looked surprised, for she smiled tensely at me in profile. She had her Lanvin headscarf on, with the signature showing, and her dark glasses.

I went over to stand beside her, but she turned away from me and started walking on ahead. After that it was maybe a couple of minutes till I was close enough to see her properly. She couldn't help walking past me at that point, and then – she slowly removed her dark glasses – she showed me just what he'd done to her.

One half of her face was blue with bruises. Her nose was swollen up. There were marks like cuts on her neck. It hadn't been a smile after all which she'd given me, because I made out that her top lip was puffed out and twisted and had been bleeding.

I couldn't really believe it. I was too shocked to find anything to say, to know how to cry even.

She walked past me, blowing smoke to vainly hide the damage.

She wasn't beautiful any more – and it was for ever now. It was all I could think. He'd killed her beauty and she wasn't any more my beautiful mother I could forgive for whatever she did to me.

While I watched she slid on the gravel and tottered and went over on her heel. I saw now she didn't belong to me. After that she couldn't get it right, the poise, the balance, the elegant patrician's disdain for the world. I heard her sniffing through her swollen nose as she rummaged in her bag for a handkerchief. What the world thought simply hadn't mattered, hadn't been allowed to. Now that resistance too, with her looks, had been beaten out of her.

Then I did want to cry. They were difficult, dry tears when they came, pricked out of me. I think she noticed, because she stuffed the handkerchief back into her bag and breathed in for a long time on her cigarette and made a lot of smoke. I was so fascinated too by her mutilations that I felt compelled to look and I was ashamed I did.

She seemed to realize, and between smoke clouds, with her face three-quarters turned to me, she let me look. This is your excellent father's doing, she was wanting me to know. She pitied me maybe for the sake of the woman I would be one day? You've seen everything men have given me: my father, your father, the callers who dropped jewels in my lap because jewels were all they had to give me.

Here we were. We were in Bavaria – we were in the fairy tale, inside it, ringed by sparkling mountains, among the patchwork meadows and the evergreen forests – but she'd travelled here just to find what she'd thought she would never have to see again: high-hedged Dorset, hump-hilled Oxfordshire, the week-end winds blasting Aldeburgh and spewing spray and froth down the windows.

Perhaps she'd really been telling the barber that she would never be back to *those* places again and doing this thing, substituting Prague, it was going to be the magical solution to everything, to our situation?

Or am I presuming too much, that she truly did have the intention in her head of reforming herself when she reached the train's destination? – and meeting my father half-way would be meant as some symbolic ritual of the heart, a kind of purification?

(In that case, why had she brought the jewels with her? – or was her real purpose to admit to my father that this was how it was, confront him with it, the state of their marriage in the icy winter of 1963? This was how we lived now?)

She looked at me through the coils of smoke. I couldn't adjust my face into a smile, not for her: not for someone I didn't know. There was nothing now. She looked at me for ages and still I didn't smile. I thought time had stopped. I remember wondering if I might 'revert', if I might turn savage because I'd been abandoned.

Through the night I'd dreamed of Hansel and Gretel lost in the forest, stumbling on the witch in her gingerbread house. I didn't fully understand then, and not for many years: for the two of them the witch was me, I was the terror in both their lives, in me their panic and guilt met and were turned by a horrible alchemy to hate.

They hated me.

Even standing there I dimly perceived it, and I was so frightened I started shaking.

My mother drew impatiently on her cigarette and blew the smoke out quickly. I couldn't control myself, my shoulders wouldn't keep still. Under her headscarf she was unknown to me. She'd been so beautiful once. Once-upon-a-time: *then* had been the magical age, the fairy tale life, if only I'd known. ('Beautiful': with her it's a word I can't describe or explain, anything I say is an abstraction and an evasion. I could try to remember her how she was, before he mutilated her, and make an Identikit face – sea-grey eyes, arch eyebrows, that pared mouth, the sculpted neck left bare, her auburn hair – and say that men lost their heads because of how she looked: but what I can't do is explain why a daughter she cared nothing for should want to restore her splendour to her and admit that she approached perfection in any part of her being.)

And, I was also thinking, what if she never recovers and every day is just like this one? She stared at me as if she was blaming me – me more than the others – I was the reason it had happened. Me. *Me.*

Now I couldn't stop crying and my tears wet my coat and I didn't care what she thought. I saw her when I could make out shapes, just staring.

I couldn't move. Everything through my tears is as clear too as if I had a photograph of it. The treacherous, overly-blue sky, a bird preening itself on a telegraph pole, the red road behind my mother as straight as an arrow for miles, the two edges of the pine forest meeting at a right angle like the walls of a massive oblong.

In the end my father had to come for me; he took me by the shoulders and steered me gently towards the car. He closed the door behind me and leaned over from the front to press the lever down to lock it. I wasn't crying any more, and I put my head back on the leather, tired to death.

The engine snarled, and the car jumped. I listened to the wheels turning under us and the gravel churning and the little chips rattling around inside the wheel arches. I looked up through the back window and imagined all that waste of azure sky like a harmless summer sea.

It began after a hundred yards, even before we'd reached the solid green geometry of forest. I had my head back and was inhaling the pine: I recognized the smell from disinfectants but, seeping into the car, it seemed to have a thinner, more sourish tang.

'We'll need the maps,' my father said. 'Have you got them?'

' "We'll need the maps",' my mother repeated him. The words sounded bloated. ' "Have you got them?" '

'Well?' he asked her impatiently, changing up gear. '*Have* you got them?'

' "Have you got them, *please*?" ' she blurted out with her broken mouth.

'Christ!' My father's fingers clutched at the wheel. 'Christ, I'm not a child, Laura!'

'Oh, I'm sorry!' She tried to say it airily. 'Pardon me, it must be the way you behave . . .'

(How, I was thinking, how is she finding so much courage to cross him?)

'The way *I* behave?'

'Tantrums –'

'Christ Almighty, what about you?'

'Yes?' She spoke slowly. 'What *about* me?'

My mother turned her head and just stared at my father – stared at him with her bruised face and twisted mouth – as if she was wishing he could be struck down dead.

He couldn't say the words, not at once.

'So superior . . .'

' "Superior"?' she repeated him. She turned her head away again. 'I should have thought . . . I should have thought that's what you require.'

' "Require" *what*?' he snapped back, grabbing at the gear knob.

My mother spelt it out, without deigning to look at him.

'Dom-in-a-tion.'

'*What*?' My father laughed, but sounded angry. 'Who says? Where did you read that crap?'

'I needn't remind you –' my mother pulled at the knot of her scarf ' – we have a child in the car.'

'All this "domination" shit –'

'I said –'

'I know what you said,' my father sniped. 'You're such a

saint, aren't you? White as snow, bloody plaster-cast saint. So above it all!'

'If you say –'

My father slammed his hand down on the dashboard.

'Above it all *fuck!*'

My mother covered her ears. Still driving, my father pulled away her right arm.

'*I'll* tell you what you are. Listen to this!'

'I'm not going to be sworn at –'

She reached for the door handle but my father wedged her left arm against the door with his weight and fastened his fingers on the other wrist.

'I only *say* it, Laura!'

'Don't talk to me!'

'I don't do it. You *do* it, Laura.'

She screwed up her face.

'Because you *can't*,' she hissed. 'You can't do *anything*.'

She spat at him, into his face.

My father watched the road, still clutching the wheel. He smiled, as if he was savouring the insult.

'That's it, Laura! That's it!'

'Bastard!'

'Language, Laura!'

'Go to hell!'

'Oh, but we are – that's exactly where we're going . . .'

The fingers of his free hand tightened on her wrist. The car rocked. My mother squirmed.

'Get – *off* – me!'

'You . . .' he twisted her wrist – 'you bloody whore!'

She jumped, let out a little scream.

'What do you think *you* are?' she spluttered.

'Tell me, Laura, suppose you tell me – and I'll tell you what *you* are. All your whoring –'

'Piss off! You've never given me *any*thing –'

The blood was running into my father's face. It turned it crimson, then – in seconds – purple.

'What did you say?'

He shook her and the car wobbled.

'Go to hell!'

'What did you say?'

The teeth rattled in her head.

'Take – take your bloody –'

'*Tell me*!'

'*I*'ll tell you.' She was shouting. '*I*'ll tell you.' She wrenched her wrist free. 'You're not a husband. You can't do anything.' She was yelling hysterically. 'You've never given me a single thing – *any*thing –'

I didn't know what she meant: how could I? I was ten years old, I'd had a privileged life. It was the way she said those things that I hated. And her laugh that started, like a cackle, like mad Mrs Rochester's up in the attic . . .

I shut my eyes against the sky, knowing what would happen.

'Slow down, will you?' my mother cried out. 'You're going too fast.'

I felt the wheels gathering speed under us, and my father told her above the wailing of the engine he would drive at whatever speed he chose, thank you very much; it was *his* car, *he* was driving it, he didn't need . . .

But I put my hands over my ears so I didn't have to hear the rest. That wasn't enough to blot it out, of course. He called my mother 'whore' and 'slut' again, in front of me.

'*I*'ll bloody decide,' he shouted at her.

I opened my eyes and looked forward, uncorking my ears.

They'd stopped wrestling, I saw, and they'd moved apart. My mother sat inflexible in her headscarf and dark glasses, watching straight ahead. My father's face in the mirror was a mystery again, how he'd seemed to me when I woke in the dawn half-light after Brno and that imbroglio with death at the check-point.

Now suddenly – how can I explain it? – my third eye was seeing everything.

I *knew* this time what was being fated for us, even before it could happen, I had no doubts . . .

I watched helplessly as my father's eyes fixed and glassed over. His body went stiff as if he'd been shocked. His arms locked on the wheel.

I looked through the windscreen, hypnotized. There was a hump in front of us which must have been the bridge and then I couldn't see what was beyond that.

It's the last thing I remember, the bump in the road, the bridge sign, the wheels throbbing on the road under us, the take-off so much slower than I was expecting. And then the green of forest from upside down like a slash in the sky, the genteel smashing of glass and metal ripping somewhere like the most normal of sounds that bright crisp winter's morning.

3

They had to use acetylene torches to get me out.

The sparks reminded me of something. Somewhere else.

I could hear birds singing on the telegraph wires. I looked, and the poles seemed to be sticking down out of the sky, which I couldn't understand.

'Don't move!' someone said in urgent foreign-sounding English among the German voices, seeming ridiculously concerned.

I had an odd view of the world. It was like looking up to the light from a sunken sea-wreck. Things glittered up there on the surface, confounding the elements, breaking the air: words, faces, flying sparks, an indescribable heat, the chromium trim of a window frame like a porthole.

I heard those birds as if I'd never heard birds before. They trilled as if they couldn't care, as if this life going on underneath them, on the road, it was merely an unexplained adventure to them.

I think I knew before they'd carried me to the ambulance. I felt it like a last instinct.

She was dead.

They wouldn't tell me in the ambulance, but I guessed from the stretched smiles, hands closing on mine.

I was so relieved. I lay for days beneath bandages where they couldn't see, just feeding on the truth of it like sweet air.

They told me on the fourth day, or the fifth day, when the first rolls were peeled off.

'Something very sad has happened.'

The nurse who could speak English best stood awkwardly by my bed.

'I know ... my mother ...'

'You know? How do you know?'

'I can ... feel ... she's not here.'

'It's terrible,' she said. 'We are so sorry for you.'

'Yes.'

'Perhaps ... you haven't understood?'

'Oh, yes. I have. My mother is dead. She's dead,' I said. 'Quite dead.'

They wouldn't let me see a mirror – was it as a punishment for saying that? – but it wasn't bothering me if I never saw my face again.

I started thinking of my mother before the three of us got into the car at the inn, and I cried sometime on that morning of the fourth day, or the fifth.

Nothing they did could stop me. They left me, without my bandages now: it was like a second birth into the world, and I cried as a baby does, howling out all its sorrow and shame.

My father was progressing. They kept telling me, with glad smiles on their faces.

I didn't want to know. I never mentioned him and they must have presumed I was amnesiac. Even when I could get up and they offered to take me, I turned stony cold and looked out the window at the small fairy tale village on the hill, the white houses and the church with its bulbous red dome and blue Christmas lights strung across the one twisting street.

I didn't want to speak to my father, however much they would try to persuade me that I did.

'*He* would like to speak to *you*,' a doctor kept telling me. 'You must. It will help you. You have been alone for many days.'

'I speak to *you*,' I would say. (It was always the same conversation we had.) 'I don't want to speak to anyone else.'

'He is your father.'

'I can't speak to my mother,' I would tell him.

'No. No, we are very sorry ...'

'So –' the logic was perfectly clear to me, inside my own head '– so I can't speak to *him* either.'

'It's not the same . . .'

'*I* think it is. It *is* the same.'

They told each other – I heard them: it seemed to be said in broken English, and conspiring, I thought, their voices were whispers – I was 'suffering the effects' and I would 'come round' in the end.

Every day I would have the same conversation (or so I remember it, as never changing) with the same smiling nurse. I gave her the benefit of my thousand doubts and thought she did it only to practise her English pronunciation, how Inge used to make a performance of practising hers.

'Wouldn't you like to see your father now?'

'Why?'

'Because he is your father! And he would like to say something to you.'

'I don't want to hear.'

'You *must*!'

'You don't know that. You can't know that.'

'Don't you have something to say to him?'

'I couldn't say it.'

'But you want to see him? You will be able to say it then?'

'No . . .'

'You can have a talk.'

'No . . .'

'*Some*time you will have to!'

'I don't *have* to. Now I can do anything I like.'

'It has been very difficult for you. But you will get better soon. Your face will get better.'

'I don't care.'

'You *have* to care. Look, it was an accident. A bad accident. But everything else goes on. And soon you will be with your father again.'

'No, no . . .'

'But you must!'

'Everything is different now!'

'Nothing —'

'*Everything*!'

When I looked up one afternoon I saw him — my father — balanced on his toes peering in through the circle of ribbed glass window in my door. My screams must have carried all through the hospital. Even when the nurses covered my mouth with their hands. Particularly then, because I bit their fingers and once I swear I even tasted bone.

I was making my point and they couldn't have ignored it. At long last I think they realized it was for real, this madness in me.

Long way east of Tuinol Town and Valium Valley there's a place of no hope left and every quack and medicineman that ever was lives there. When you've been there long enough and you won't die they give you a map, all cut up into tiny pieces, and they send you out with smiles on the terrible long way home. It's called the Librium Drive, and it's hell, and I wouldn't wish it on anybody.

I was dazed, out for the count. So much about that time I can only surmise.

A cousin of my mother's flew over from Cumberland. I looked up one afternoon and she was standing over me, a hugely able hurricane of a woman — with her daughter Abigail behind her (the name floated over to me), who was watching me timidly and stricken with awe.

Another day it began snowing, and I re-surfaced. Quite heavily it snowed: I woke with the soft thuds on the window. I watched little drifts gather in the corner of the sill. The village on its knoll shimmered across the valley like lights through water.

I watched and I lay wondering if *this* was what my mother had meant. I was hearing those words she'd said to the barber, and I forgot the impulse which had made her say them. She began to seem inestimably brave to me, my mother. I heard her say the words, and they bloomed in my mind all that day and for days afterwards, like the flowers – the yellow roses – I'd woken to find beside my bed, standing in cold fresh water.

I thought of Prague. I thought of Salzburg. I thought of the streets of London turning underfoot to slush.

I rallied. I hugged my knees to my chest, like an embryo, laughing. I wanted to be in England – with my mother's cousin and her incredulous daughter, Abigail – in Cumberland with its fell-farms and tarns, there more than anywhere else in the world.

I thought almost nostalgically of all those impassioned duets from the lit window in the dashboard. I thought of so much travelling and all to discover three strangers, like passengers approaching in another car we might have noticed, speeding past them in the night. Illuminated for one or two moments in the sweep of our headlights. As suddenly lost again . . .

But still they wouldn't leave me, passing in and out of the room, asking me to smile when my head felt like a crystal bowl I lived inside.

'You're looking better today,' the nurse told me one morning or afternoon when the light through the window seemed stronger than usual, like a bright bulb confusing my crystal prisms. She stood at the end of my bed. 'Your aunt is here from England – and Abigail. Do you want to see them?'

Inside my glass house I said nothing.

'Also, your father has gone away now.'

' "*Gone away*"?' The glass couldn't contain my surprise, my voice echoed croakily inside it.

'He has left a letter for you.' It was held up in front of me, a white oblong envelope which seemed illuminated too. 'Here it is. Would you like me to open it for you?'

'No,' my voice said.

'I can read it to you.'

156

'No,' I heard myself repeat. 'No, thank you.'

'Where shall I leave it?' The nurse looked for a clear surface somewhere within my reach. 'Then you can read it for yourself.'

I smelt the starch of her white uniform as the envelope was held up again in front of my eyes, so it had the proof of my own two eyes.

'He's used your full name, do you see? "Annoele Bennett Tomlinson". It can only be for you.'

The white oblong disappeared out the corner of one eye.

'Was that your mother's name? "Bennett"?'

'Yes.'

'So you will always have that,' she said. 'It will remind you of her. All your life.'

'Yes,' I said.

I didn't know if it would or not.

I smelt the yellow roses as the vase was moved.

'Is "Annoele" a common name in England?'

'No,' I said. My voice sounded dispirited.

'It must mean you are an unusual person.'

'It just means . . .' I thought, '. . . it just means . . . no one else has my name.' I thought again. 'You have to say it twice for people. They've never heard of it.'

'At least they remember your name.'

'I don't think *that*'s why they remember me,' I said.

I screwed up my eyes against the shrill light from outside.

'Where's he gone?' I asked.

'Your father? I suppose, to where he works.'

'Prague?'

'Yes.'

'He said that?'

'No, he didn't say. But he was . . . anxious not to stay here.'

'He hasn't gone to London?'

'I don't know. Perhaps he would have said if he was going to London.'

'Don't you know where to?'

157

'There is his letter.' The nurse pointed. 'Don't you want to open it?'

I didn't open it.

The letter was lost afterwards. Maybe my 'aunt' took it, or the police claimed it, but I never had the courage to ask during those years when I was being brought up with Abigail.

So I don't know what it was he had to tell me. If he was confessing to me, that he'd meant to kill my mother – and so himself too, and me.

He was dead to me now, quite dead, as my mother was dead.

I sometimes think *I* didn't survive either. We are three ghosts, who couldn't endure beyond our moment of most intense life.

It ended in a split second's anger. There was the bump in the road ahead of us, and no more territory left for my mother and father to fight over, no more pride to be snatched. I was forgotten, as I always had been – they were fighting their final war.

It was meant to be an end, so there could be no victor this time. And hadn't my mother told me, as the train carrying us east succumbed to the soft white might of the drifting snow, things had been against us all the way . . .

4

DIPLOMAT DISAPPEARS

A British diplomat has failed to return to his post at an embassy in Eastern Europe.

Officials in London admit that they are anxious to locate him. Security organizations in several countries have been alerted.

It is certain that the diplomat is the same one whose wife died a fortnight ago as the result of a holiday motoring tragedy in southern Germany.

The man vanished from a hospital where he was being treated. He received fractures and bruises in the accident. His daughter, who is still in care, sustained more serious injuries, principally to her face and neck. According to the latest bulletin her condition is much more comfortable and she is now making a rapid recovery.

There is speculation that the diplomat, an attaché, may be experiencing the effects of amnesia.

A medical expert said yesterday that, in his opinion, it is 'highly unlikely' that the diplomatic envoy reported as missing has lost his memory, as newspapers have claimed in recent days.

Last night police surprised officials and reporters at Heathrow Airport by cordoning off Arrival Gate 7 at BEA's terminal just minutes before a Comet carrying sixty-four passengers was scheduled to arrive from Munich.

On board was the daughter of Mr Simon Tomlinson, whose wife was killed recently in a car accident in Bavaria. A report and photograph were carried in our 28 December edition.

Mr Tomlinson is an attaché at the British Embassy in Prague.

A zoom-lens catches the tearful agony of pretty little Ann-noele Tomlinson.

An air hostess holds her hand to lead her from the plane.

She had travelled on the BEA flight from Germany with her aunt.

A police security ring prevented reporters from talking to the pair.

Interest is mounting in Fleet Street about the involvement of Scotland Yard in the affair of her father's disappearance.

Mr Simon Tomlinson, 38, is a senior official at our embassy in Prague.

The lonely beat of two constables outside the Kensington home of Mr Simon Tomlinson, the Foreign Office 'mandarin' who has failed to return to take up his duties at the British Embassy in Prague.

Little Ann-noele Tomlinson holds her aunt's hand as she arrives to begin another term at the exclusive school she attends in central London (fees £216 a term). A policewoman looks on helpfully.

After calls from two Opposition MPs in the House of Commons on Wednesday night demanding that information be made public concerning allegations of possible misconduct by a high-ranking Intelligence expert at a British embassy in an East European country, a spokesman at the Defence Department admitted yesterday that the diplomat is not expected to be back at his post 'within the foreseeable future'.

A police official issued the following statement late yesterday afternoon: 'The investigations we are pursuing concerning a person or persons named in certain newspapers are of a merely routine kind. All personnel engaged in sensitive Intelligence work affecting the national good expect to come under scrutiny from time to time.'

Last night the Ministry of Defence confirmed recent news-paper statements that the senior British diplomat who failed to report back to an East European embassy after winter leave is now being sought for questioning by officers from New Scotland Yard and the Intelligence services, on 'certain matters of public concern'.

According to reports, these investigations are said to be 'of a highly delicate and involved nature'. Possible breaches of national security have been suggested.

The Ministry representative announced that requests for a press conference are being considered. He refused to name the diplomat, whose identity has been established in newspaper coverage of events during the past two weeks.

Yesterday afternoon members of the Press Corps were summoned to a briefing at the Foreign Office. A prepared communiqué was delivered, which we reproduce in full:

'Investigations are being conducted by appointed police and H.M. Government agencies into an alleged breach of national security.

Confirmation is hereby given to press reports that a Counsellor currently attached to a British legation in an East European capital is being sought for questioning.

We would welcome tact and moderation from the press and radio and television authorities in dealing with a sensitive matter which, if misrepresented, is likely to cause alarm to British subjects and overseas governments alike.

Bulletins will be issued as necessary by the Foreign Office to accredited press agencies and to radio and television news departments. These bodies are advised that no further information should be elicited at the present time from this or any other official source.'

SPY FEVER!
News Clamp-Down
Inside sources say that supremos at the Foreign Office

are 'seething' about a new Communist infiltration of British Intelligence personnel who hold official posts in Eastern Europe. The hunt is on for the missing envoy at the British Embassy in Prague, named in Monday's edition, only weeks after a leak of information is believed to have occurred concerning the secret strategic plans of NATO land-forces.

The Government is anxious to halt further speculation, as the tone of a spokesman's statement at yesterday's news-briefing suggested.

But it does not stop us asking this question:
HOW MANY MORE SPIES HAVE WE GOT ON THE TAXPAYERS' PAYROLL?

The Great British Public are entitled to answers: just WHERE IS IT ALL GOING TO END?

Concern was expressed in Parliament last night by Government backbenchers on the matter of possible press interference in the Tomlinson affair.

Mr Archibald Gray MP said that 'irresponsible reporting' by newspaper and magazine journalists and the 'general complicity of Fleet Street editors' are bound to have prejudiced current investigations by police and Military Intelligence.

Opposition MP Mr Eric Tovey declared that it was true that investigations had been hindered, but the cause was Government indecision. He claimed that both Intelligence experts and New Scotland Yard officers were acting under direct instructions from the Foreign Office and that there had been too much 'soft-pedalling' among Government 'brass hats' in Whitehall. Mr Tovey told the House that newspapers had returned some urgency to the matter: it was because of their continued pressure that the Foreign Office had finally been prepared to admit the man's identity. Tomlinson, he said, was 'a member of the Old Boy system in Whitehall'. Mr Tovey added that, while details of the diplomat's recent activities had

*not been disclosed, informed sources were now freely specu-
lating that they may amount to 'treason'.*

A wedding photograph of the lovely young bride of debonair
Simon Richard Welch Tomlinson, whose continuing disappearance threatens to expose another espionage scandal.

The former Laura Bennett, a vicar's daughter from a pic-
ture-postcard village in Dorset, was tragically killed in a car
crash when the Jaguar saloon her husband was driving went
out of control on a German country road.

It is now known that high-level tip-offs in Munich and Bonn
were responsible for the involvement of investigators acting on
behalf of the British Government. They flew out on a mystery
flight from London within hours of Mr Tomlinson absconding
from hospital and immediately began extending the scope of
local police enquiries.

It has been reckoned that it was costing smooth-talking fugi-
tive diplomat Simon Tomlinson a minimum of £200 a week to
foot the bills of his wife's glamorous jet-set existence in
Kensington.

Was that the mistake he made? – living too well?

Mrs Laura Tomlinson, a striking beauty, did not accompany
her husband on his postings. Neighbours say that the couple
met only occasionally.

A friend told us, 'Mrs Tomlinson was more concerned that
her daughter should have a proper home-life in London.'

'Mrs Tomlinson loved parties,' a neighbour said yesterday.
'She loved life.'

The Foreign Office has refused to comment on a claim in
a newspaper yesterday that, for two years prior to his disappearance, Mr Simon Tomlinson's movements had been
under surveillance. It is stated in the article that for at least
eighteen months, until last August, Mr Tomlinson's house in
London was kept under close police scrutiny and that during

that period trained 'monitoring' agents of Military Intelligence departments posed as selected staff and tradesmen.

The reporter who has made these allegations blames the authorities for negligence and delay in following up the first reports of the fatal car accident, which appeared in the Fleet Street press in the final few days of December.

5

In 1982 some cancer-scare stories 'broke' about the Christmas Island explosions in the mid-1950s.

Men and women diagnosed as 'terminal' were appearing on tea-time television with drawn, sickly faces to tell of their fates, sometimes prompted by passive children who had inherited genetic disorders. We heard eye-witness accounts – about heat blasting the skin like a blow-torch, about a light so intense filling the day that you could see the bones in your hand.

The interviewers spoke in urgent, committed voices. A design studio's abstract of a mushroom cloud filled a corner of the screen. There were cases cited of children having been born with webbed feet; one baby girl who hadn't lived longer than a week had had no bones in her face.

It was very 'worthy' news, of course. But the story over-worked itself, the presentation came across as too hysterical for early-evening viewing. The sufferers I saw being interviewed were not the simple victims of random chance but either technicians who'd been adequately paid for their services or – filmed not in cramped living rooms where the camera lingered on prancing glass animals and china ladies in hoop-skirts, but posed against slubbed silk wallpaper or a garden pergola – the appointed government watchers like my father, who'd been determined young men in the 1950s with ambition and drive and their futures to make.

*   *   *

'It's sad, Abigail, they don't have music any more in restaurants. I didn't even know if there *was* a Bendicks still.'

'Did you mind, coming here?'

'Mind it? Why should I mind? I don't get the chance much.'

'I couldn't have your life.'

'It's not glamorous, being a journalist, not at all.'

'No. No, I didn't mean that. It's just . . . I have to stay in my own place, with my own things. It's a tug for me coming to London even. I'm very dull, amn't I?'

'It's strange being here again. I don't recognize anything about it, only the name. There's no music. The decor used to be darker: fumed oak. But it's where we came. Maybe this is where we sat.'

'Why do you do it, Annoele? Always this search. It's history now.'

'Or that table, over there? No. No, *this* one.'

'It wasn't.'

'What?'

'No. You sat in the middle of the room. Where everyone could see you.'

'I'm wrong, then? I'm wrong, am I, Abigail? The past, it doesn't surrender itself so easily after all, does it?'

'I don't follow you . . .'

'I do wonder about it sometimes, why should I have become a journalist, why that?'

'You've seen the world, when you were a child . . .'

'I saw the insides of cars. I lived in hotels. "Foreign people" were there to serve us: we three served *their* curiosity.'

'But you noticed things?'

'My nerves were raw. I was petrified we were going to make a scene. I was more conservative than my parents were. I lived for the right and true "middle way". Doing the proper thing and being seen to do it. Causing no shame, wishing no harm done.'

'You became a journalist because . . . because you wanted to tell the truth to people?'

'But that's what *I don't* do, Abigail. Not at all. I've thought about it, I've thought about it so often.

'Anything I write, I present, that's *my* view of a situation. Do you see?

'Look – maybe someone tells me lies, I can know they're lies, technically. But they're the truth of that person's vision, indirectly – their stance, their politics. *Do* you see? They can be *sincere* lies or . . . or just bloody-minded evasions . . . and you can't judge between them. The "truth" there has something to do with *not* the truth. And I have to decide what.'

'But that's what you do – you balance up, don't you? Till you find a fair picture?'

'A picture that's fair to *me*. It's only *my* reputation I'm trying to save – every time it is.'

'You're doing yourself down, Annoele.'

'And another thing, you think it's "freedom" that takes you winging to wherever you're going. It's a woman's "right" to have a job like mine, and to have her independence. It's the freedom that comes from living in a democracy which allows you to say what you believe is at the heart of a matter.'

'Well, these aren't figments, are they? They're real, they're truths . . .'

'They have to be defended, constantly. The more of them you have, the more you need to be on your guard. Vigilant, protective. It makes you jealous, all that watching, maybe narrow-minded in some ways. It closes you in. Maybe you start to lose the track . . .'

'I meant us to be having a nice afternoon tea, Annoele. I meant us to be enjoying ourselves – in Bendicks, you said, for old times' sake, "if it's there". And here we are, and we're getting very gloomy.'

'Yes, maybe that *is* the table, over there. And *that*'s where we sat.'

'I know it was.'

'You "*know*"? How?'

'An accident. I was with my mother. We both saw you. One Christmas time. You seemed to me to be "Bendicks people": very exotic, I thought. Your mother was so beautiful.'

' "Beautiful" –'

'She was wearing a mink coat – and a velvet beret, olive-green velvet – and she had a crocodile bag.'

'Crocodile – alligator – lizard – seal – kid. She had a leopard-skin jacket too, you know. My mother was a killer.'

'I remember seeing you both. I thought you looked so elegant, both of you. You had a coat with a velvet collar. You both looked . . . unreal. I felt we were so staid by comparison.'

'What did we say to you?'

'We just looked. Gazed. Admired. From afar. My mother was going to – say something. I think she was frightened *your* mother wouldn't recognize her, or want to. Well . . . your mother . . .'

'You don't need to say it.'

'They were just cousins. And it wasn't enough, maybe. I don't know. It wasn't enough to take us across the room. That would have been *our* "journey". To me, you were both further away than across a room.'

'And here I am. Not so advantaged; not so blessed. As you can see.'

'You were, for me. You always were. The circumstances made you that person. The circumstances now, they're not the same.'

'I used to think we . . . I can't explain it very well, we embellished, we ornamented other people's existences. I honestly used to think that.'

'But you *did*!'

'We gave people something they didn't have themselves. Maybe they thought we lived lives of perfect happiness. We fulfilled their wishes. Their wishes for themselves. *Us*!'

'You mustn't –'

'It was what they *saw*, it was what they wanted to see. Afterwards . . .'

'Your father, you mean? The newspapers . . .'

'That really was the end. The reporters ringing the doorbell, standing waiting outside the school gates . . . No, I meant, when they couldn't see, when we weren't on display. When my mother was still alive.'

'We drove past your house once. I couldn't believe you lived in all of it.'

'It couldn't have been big enough to keep us apart. Or my mother and my father, when he came.'

'It *looked* –'

'I found photographs of them both in my father's old trunk in the attic, did I ever tell you?'

'I don't *remember* you telling me –'

'From the time before they were married – I suppose they hadn't met yet.'

'What did you discover?'

' "Discover"? Oh. Only that they were like two utterly different and separate people. Both sets of photographs had nothing to do with each other. So it seemed to me. It was as if it was an accident they were in the same attic at all.'

'What was in them? In the photographs?'

'They were with their friends. My mother was with hers – young men, "blades" – I didn't recognize any of them. My father stood about with other men, *his* friends. It just made it more difficult for me to understand why they *did* marry, you see. Coming from their different worlds.

'That smarmy couple who gave us sex lessons at St Neots on Friday afternoons – do you remember? – the wife (she said she was) in those tight Bardot dresses, and the man wearing his baggiest trousers and standing with his hands deep in his pockets – they were right after all and we only sniggered at them. Without "respect", they said, it's "an act of darkness". What I think they meant was, you risk being destroyed by what you create if you create it – not "cruelly", but "without . . .– "without *love*".'

*　　*　　*

It's a complicated story of coincidence how I discovered that he was in the Aegean and not where I presumed he must be, and how I managed to set about tracking him down to one island and to one town. What matters is that in the end I *did* find him.

I returned to the island a second time, from Athens where I'd arranged to work on an archaeological story, about a famous British excavator of Edwardian times with many skeletons rattling in his cupboard.

I flew there, in one of the little propeller-driven planes of 1950s vintage which were operating then on the route. It was an unnerving journey through mist and fine rain. The landing on the grassy airstrip was unannounced – the nose suddenly went veering downwards – and bumpy.

From the taxi I noticed several new hotels, a holiday Beach Klub with thatched huts, a few discos and drinking dens with flashing neon signs. I didn't quite know what I'd come back to.

On a walkabout I realized very quickly what had happened: the town had become a haven for gays, men and women of the homosexual beau monde.

In the nightclubs the clothes were fluorescent-bright and year-round tans glowed. Everyone was open and completely uninhibited and they smiled toothpaste advertisement smiles.

We didn't 'engage' or 'connect', those people and I, not at all. Theirs was a particular morality of behaviour for a par-ticular epoch: it ignored me, it ignored those who existed out of its scope by experience or attitude.

I was reminded of the swinging sixties – but this was swing-ier, and wilder. Secrecy had no part in their lives, it was exorcised, it was other people's hang-up now.

This was perfect freedom, but I noticed too how the eyes were never done hunting; it was the predatory skills of the caveman they'd re-employed in their quest for perfect sex.

I waited till the next morning before I set out for the cottage in the fields.

I hoped I might see him in the streets, that I might catch a flicker of recognition for the woman who'd knocked him off his balance on a morning like this one, five years before.

But I didn't see him. And his house didn't look how I remembered it. It was newly painted, and there were a couple of mopeds parked outside.

I was standing putting off time, debating what to do, when the door opened and a group of middle-aged and younger men emerged – holidaymakers, in sawn-off jeans and fashionable pink or lemon T-shirts. Two mounted the mopeds and got them to splutter to life, then sped off.

The rest came down the lane, walking towards me. They spoke German. They looked happy and relaxed, with their day open-ended in front of them. When I asked my question in their language, they were very polite: they said they were sorry but they couldn't help me with what I wanted to know.

I also asked in two or three shops. About the Englishman.

He'd gone, they could tell me that much, but no one had an idea where to. I found the address of the holiday accommodation agency who now owned the house: they put me on to the land agent: he told me the Englishman had sold the house because he wanted to leave the town.

'Where is he now? Do you know?'

The man patted his stomach and shook his head.

'Somewhere near the town?'

Another shake of the head. No, he was sorry, he didn't know that either, lady.

No one remembered how the furniture had been transported. It seemed incredible to me that a life could be lost sight of so easily. I went and asked my questions of the owner of the taverna where he'd spent so much time, but with no more success. A different owner now, I discovered, who called it the Poseidon Quick-Grill ('As Seen in *The Dark Side of the Sun*'), a fiery-faced man proud of his modern notions, who let me know he wasn't at all inclined to talk of the distant past.

He'd just vanished.

I even tackled the priest on the subject. He didn't speak English, so I had to find an interpreter, a holy-looking school-girl who turned her head away from me to revere the old man. He said he had no knowledge of the Englishman's where-abouts. 'Are you family?' he asked in his own language – but it seemed to me too long a story to begin, so I muttered 'ochi' with my lips and shook my head.

He'd moved on, obviously. His travels weren't over yet. Maybe it was to a village up in the hills? – but since he hadn't been seen, more likely it was to another island. Was it this island's new character which had alarmed him – offended him even, with its homosexual fame? Or might he have been needing medical attention? Perhaps he hadn't completed his journey, and he hasn't yet? – or did his journey finish for him, but in another place and without him ever reaching where he was bound for?

6

Sometimes I think it was like a travesty of the Christmas narrative. Our 'flight' and the misadventures that befell us. But we had no stars – only the glinting rain-runs on the Jaguar's windows, which could have been confused for stars shining. That was all. Not so wise, either: and the gifts were of our own desiring.

I occasionally hear the music. Not the carols. The other songs of loneliness I listened to when my mother played them on the radiogram in my father's house, when her guests had gone. Anthony Newley, Alma Cogan, Julie London. They get to me – like dank afternoons with the sky the colour of old florins, when the year is running down, in winter.

Now the songs are kitsch: and *we*, with our outrageous past, have become . . . harmless almost.

Not so harmless as the cancer-scare stories on television. I hear 'Christmas Island' spoken of, and twice the name 'Simon Tomlinson' has been listed among those of the able young observers who were appointed by the government of the day. Somehow I never conceived of things ending for him in a cancer ward. That's the part of history you can't help, which has you its victim. What got us into the newspapers and had our story lining drawers and wardrobes and propping up the wobbly legs of tables and wrapping fish and chips.

History – so Inge told me when the man came to fix my mother's television set, who couldn't have been a television repair man after all since Inge wasn't who we thought she was either – history is also what is personal to you: not merely the bald facts I trained myself to memorize from my school books, and the even balder facts about the Tomlinson family that

173

came out when the Fleet Street scavengers got to work. 'There is only one history of importance, and it is the history of what you once believed in, and what you came to believe in . . .' It must be that we merit *some* control. I still ask myself, couldn't we have been better, happier people if only . . . ? If only . . .

I looked for other things – 'wonder' and 'faith' – when that was impossible, because 'love' was missing: simple and not-so-simple 'love'. All those wars I watched on television night after night – the Korean, the Algerian, the Congolese one, the Cuban war that nearly was, the mechanical eyes turning in the sky. All those love-songs on the car radio, and we never knew what they meant in our age of abject faithlessness. The silver leaping Jaguar devouring the road . . .

We lost love long before our journey began that winter to Prague. It was lost before I was born, perhaps on another journey – a schoolgirl's on the milk-train home from London to Dorset, or a student's hitch from the lesser end of Surbiton up to Cambridge in its fen haar. Love was forgotten, as easily as a glove is dropped or a hat mislaid, on a taxi ride across London in 1951 from the Festival Hall to the Ritz (where angels dined) when it was the future that handsome couple had in their sights, not what they should have been able to see with their eyes, which might have warned them. But if they hadn't been so greedy to save themselves from the world they'd grown up in, then I wouldn't have been born into mine and none of this would have been . . .

When the car crashed, my father's presents for us he'd hidden in the boot went scattering all over the road. I saw them from the stretcher as they hoisted me into the back of the ambulance. How odd, I was thinking, how queer: not that they should be littering a country road in their pretty silver paper and blue ribbon tied into bows, but that we should be paying so much for them . . .

With everything we had.

RONALD FRAME

WALKING MY MISTRESS IN DEAUVILLE

Comprising a novella and nine short stories, this sparkling collection explores relationships between the sexes from a variety of often surprising angles. From the first awkward sexual awareness of youth to the ritual dances of courtship and the delicate betrayals of marriage, Ronald Frame lets no shade of emotion or sign of deception escape his razor-sharp, playful eye.

'As always, Frame offers masterful subtlety in his plots and characterisation, and varies his vantage point ingeniously'
The Daily Telegraph

'Clearly the work of an author developing into practised maturity . . . his ability to represent a wide range of characters, of either sex, is prodigious'
The Guardian

'The novella is gripping, the best piece of narrative that Mr Frame has written . . . He perpetually brings you up against the otherness of other people, their ultimate unknowability'
The Scotsman

'An enjoyably unpredictable collection'
Today

'It is good to see Ronald Frame in such fine form . . . the cumulative effect is exhilarating'
Scotland on Sunday